经典全译版

〔美〕托马斯·潘恩◎著

周喜峰　李静宇◎译

Common Sense

民主与建设出版社　博集天卷
CS-BOOKY

图书在版编目（CIP）数据

常识：经典全译版 /（美）潘恩（Paine, T.）著；周喜峰，李静宇译. —北京：民主与建设出版社，2015.10

书名原文：Common Sense

ISBN 978-7-5139-0847-4

Ⅰ.①常… Ⅱ.①潘… ②周… ③李… Ⅲ.①政治思想史－美国－近代 Ⅳ.①D097.124

中国版本图书馆CIP数据核字（2015）第244176号

常识：经典全译版

出 版 人	许久文
著 者	[美]托马斯·潘恩
译 者	周喜峰 李静宇
责任编辑	李保华
出版发行	民主与建设出版社有限责任公司
电 话	（010）59419779
社 址	北京市朝阳区阜通东大街融科望京产业中心B座601室
邮 编	100102
印 刷	北京嘉业印刷厂
版 次	2015年10月第1版　2015年10月第1次印刷
开 本	787mm×1092mm　1/32
字 数	102千字
印 张	6.5
书 号	ISBN 978-7-5139-0847-4
定 价	25.00元

注：如有印、装质量问题，请与出版社联系。

目 录 CONTENTS

编者序 我说段历史，你可别激动啊 001

再版序言 019

第一章 概论政府的起源和目的 & 简评英格兰政体 001

第二章 论君主政体与世袭 013

第三章 对美洲当下情况的思考 031

第四章 论美洲目前的能力，附带一些杂感 063

附言 083

编者序

我说段历史，你可别激动啊

《常识》之于我们，就像《明朝那些事儿》之于美国人，虽然可能很有趣，但背景知识就像一只拦路虎。我们会觉得《明朝》就是那些简简单单的事儿，美国人会觉得《常识》真的是常识，但换了位置就完全不一样了。所以我们干了两件事。第一就是在正文里加了一些注释，在每颗老虎牙旁边都放一把钳子。第二就是在这里说一下历史背景，一段激动人心的历史。

那时候的北美大陆，还没有一个叫作美国的国家。这里是13个殖民区，英法两国争夺这里的控制权，打了七年，所以叫"七年战争"。后来英国赢了，北美就成了大英帝国的一个海外行省，所以人们护照上的国籍是英国人，服从伦敦调遣，为英皇尽忠，有作为大英帝国一部分的家族自豪感。

打仗需要花钱，花费大量的钱。英国在欢呼胜利的同时，尴尬地发现，七年的战争耗空了国家，大英帝国的财政捉襟见肘。英国把目光转向了抢回来的小妾，企图让它做牛做马，也就是把军费转嫁给它。英国用了三招：倾销剩余产品（美洲只能进口英国产品，卖不动的英国产品都弄这儿来卖）、独占原料供给（木材等只能卖给英国，由英国定价）、课收重税。前两项倒没什么，因为还有家族自豪感在那里顶着，但这第三条政策把美洲人惹毛了。

1765年英国议会通过了针对美洲的《印花税法案》，一下子多征四十多种税。美洲人一下子就蒙了，突然发现了自己作为二等公民的地位。美洲人说：我们北美洲在英国议会里没有代表，你们一群人把门一关开个会，出门就说会议决定让我们交钱，这叫什么事儿啊？北美大陆发出了"无代表不征税"的呼声，家族自豪感完全丧失。

当情感遭到背叛，必会激起仇怨。美洲人开始拒绝购买英国货物，宁愿穿纺织的粗布衣服，也不买英国的。人民频频请愿游行，甚至发生了暴力冲突。英国慌了神，立刻派兵镇压。高压之下，美洲出现了很多秘密的反英组织，比如"自由之子"等地下党。后来，美洲人的抗议实在太激烈了，英国内阁经过激烈辩论，一年后终于同意撤销《印花税法》。但是军费还是没有着落，所以还得找美洲人要一点儿。

1767年，内阁通过了新的税收法案《唐森德税法》，纸、玻璃、铅、颜料等美洲不能自产但又非常需要的东西，都要加高额进口税。首先说"进口税"这个词，一看就明白了，你是你，我是我，咱俩不是一个国家。

唐森德知道，加税后，原来一块钱的东西现在要卖两块，在垄断物品上加价，必然会引起不满，所以同时规定：税吏有权进入民宅、货栈、店铺，搜查违禁物品和走私货物。

美洲人反抗的激烈程度是唐森德始料未及的，频发暴力事件，再加上英国军队纪律松散，时时骚扰当地居民，双方关系很紧张。1770年3月5日，驻扎在波士顿的英军以保护税官为名，向抗议民众开枪，打死5个人①，史称"波士顿惨案"。这一下不得了，全美洲开始爆发武力抗法行为。殖民地越来越强烈的反抗，使英国在1770年3月废除了《唐森德税法》。但双方达成了一个妥协，那就是保留茶叶税。茶叶是一种很特殊的商品。第一，美洲本来就可以自产茶叶，不是一定买英国人的；第二，这种两国都可以产的东西，要征关税，进口的英货自然比本地货要贵，所以可以保护本地茶商和茶农；第三，保留茶叶税，可以象征性地表明英国在殖民地是有征税权的。因为茶叶很特殊，所以茶叶税得以保留，但这也为后来的冲突埋下了祸根。

1773年，为了倾销积存茶叶，英国内阁通过《救济东印度公司条例》，授予东印度公司在北美销售积压茶叶的专利权，免交进口关税。其中明令禁止殖民地人民贩卖"私茶"。

---

① 有的资料说是4个人。

为什么要专门加上这么一条？我们得看看什么是私茶，它为什么会产生。

中国从汉武帝开始，政府就会垄断几种常用物资收为官营，比如盐和铁。所有非官方经营的盐和铁，那都是私货。我记得赵雅芝在很多年前的电视剧《戏说乾隆》中，扮演盐帮帮主程淮秀，所谓盐帮，其实就是贩卖私盐的走私分子组织的帮派。

本地茶叶要交税，所以贵，所以不买，这是可以理解的。但是面对比本地茶叶便宜得多的进口茶叶，为什么不买？北美人认为，如果饮用这种茶叶，就等于默认了英国法律的合法性，所以全民抵制茶叶倾销。这就和中国抗战时期全民抵制日货是一样的，你再便宜我也不买。这时候就必然产生大量逃税的本地茶商，把价格降到和进口茶能抗衡的价位，因为免交税，所以便宜，所以是私货和违禁物。当时美洲人消费的茶叶中，有9/10都是私茶。

　　这种畸形的经济关系早晚会出问题的。1773年12月16日，塞缪尔·亚当斯带领60个人潜入商船，把价值1.5万英镑的342箱茶叶倒入大海，史称"波士顿倾茶事件"。英国认为这是对殖民当局权威的恶意挑衅。为了镇压反抗，1774年3月英国议会通过了惩罚性法令，强制性规定：英军可强行进入民宅搜查，取消马萨诸塞的自治地位，封闭北美最大的港口波士顿港。这导致了波士顿商业大面积停滞，很多人因此流离失所甚至饿死，饥饿中暴徒四起。

　　人民在抵制英国货物，地下党在秘密反英，官方在干啥？1774年9月5日~10月26日，第一届大陆会议在费城召开，要求：英国取消对殖民地的经济限制和高压法令，针对殖民地的法案必须经过殖民地人民的同意，撤走英国驻军，殖民地实行自治。如果英国不接受，北美将于12月1日起停止任何对英贸易。

　　自治就是自己治理自己，我们国家也有香港特别行政区、宁夏回族自治区等。但自治的程度有高有低，大陆会议并没有明确到底是什么程度的自治，所以这个目标就成了悬搁在空中的东西。

　　自治的前提是归属中央政府管辖。所以大陆会议秉承"国王仁慈，议会暴虐"的原则，认为恶法来自内阁，所以把希望寄托在了一个明君身上，打算绕过内阁，直接把请愿书呈交英王。会议宣称北美完全忠于王室，依附大不列颠，"有人告诉你们，说我们是叛乱的、不满政府和希望独立的，请相信，那些都不是事实……"他们只想恢复七年战争结束时的情况，也就是没有任何恶法时。

　　上面是官方意见，而驻美英军和美洲民间武装之间，一直剑拔弩张。1775年4月18日晚，800名英国轻步兵从波士顿开拔，准备开赴康科德夺取当地民兵的军需，并逮捕反英组织的首脑。组织起来的北美人民拿起武器出门迎击，第二天在莱克星顿村发生了战斗。几十个村民对抗800名正规武装士兵，寡不敌众，阵亡8人。英军扑向康科德镇，但当他们赶到时，弹药已经转移，领导人已经隐藏。指挥官一看不对劲，命令立刻撤退，这时，一排排子弹从四面八方射来。英军逃回波士顿后清点人数，损失共247人。

莱克星顿的枪声被称为美国独立战争的开始。独立战争纪念碑上是一尊手握步枪、头戴草帽的民兵，碑上刻着一段话："坚守阵地。在敌人没有射击之前，不要先开枪；但是，如果敌人硬要把战争强加在我们头上，那么，就让战争从这里开始吧！"

然后英王对美洲说：要么服从，要么毁灭。要和平还是要自由的问题，摆在了人们面前。潘恩认为，这就算撕破脸了吧。他的回答是坚决的：不自由毋宁死。但是激进的革命家和官方的态度不可能高度一致，政治家们要考虑更多的方面，这时候有三个纠缠不清的问题。第一，该不该打？也就是，以战争换自由，是否符合美洲人的利益。一开战，就得有正规军，光靠民兵肯定是不管用的，而建正规军，钱和将领的问题怎么解决？第二，如果该打，是针对英国议会发动内战，还是针对英国发起民族独立的革命战争？也就是独立不独立的问题。第三，如果民族独立了，是该建立全欧洲都仰慕的英国式君主立宪制度，还是共和国制度？

关于帝王的问题，现在看来是常识，但是当时的人们可不见得这么想，帝王还是要有的，要不那还叫什么国家？想一想王国维为什么要在清朝皇帝退位后自杀你就明白了。

1775年5月10日召开的第二届大陆会议上，本杰明·富兰克林、托马斯·杰弗逊等代表仍然对是否开战、是否独立等问题犹豫不决。

这种事情在现在看来是很荒唐的，但是先进的思想阶层可不那么想啊。光荣革命之后，整个西方都推崇英国的君主立宪政体。没有国王那叫什么国家啊？要是自己独立并产生一个国王，那不就是叛臣贼子吗？虽然大陆会议已经是一个政权组织，起着常设中央政府的作用，但谁也无法下定决心和这样一个优秀的"母国"一刀两断。

　　1775年 6月15日，大陆会议通过决议，组织大陆军，任命华盛顿为总司令。但是请注意：战争的目的不是革命，不是独立。战争的目的只是"清君侧，诛晁错"，或者说这是一场针对内阁的内战，绝对不针对国王，绝对不是要推翻王权，绝对不是要独立。国王是明君，只是为内阁所蒙蔽。1776年1月，在华盛顿坐首席的军官餐厅里，每晚都为英王的健康干杯。而约翰·亚当斯等少数政治家看到了革命和独立而不是内战。但是，他们因为种种既有利益方面的考虑不敢公开呼吁。本杰明·罗什看到潘恩付梓前的书稿，深深地被打动了，还给它起名"常识"，但自己却躲得远远的。

　　托马斯·潘恩发表的《常识》，针对当时亟待解决的几个问题进行回答。首先，应当反对的不是内阁，而是国王和君权制。君权制才是一切罪恶的来源，英王只是一头皇家畜生，貌似雄狮实为蠢驴，英国皇室的祖先只不过是个篡政的强盗头子。议会是英国政体中的共和部分，那是应当尊重的部分。《常识》一出，振聋发聩，它把战争的矛头从议会转向了国王。

其次，美国应当革命、独立，而不是展示武力，使英国忌惮妥协，因为妥协意味着毁灭。美军必然胜利，英国会妥协，但绝对不会放弃对殖民地的立法权这一宪法权力。英国暂时退让，必然是为了更猛烈地反击，而拥有对美洲的立法权则能保证它的报复会猛烈无比。《常识》刺破了黑夜的幕布，指明了战争的前景。如果没有潘恩的笔，华盛顿举起的剑，就不知道该刺向哪里了。《常识》是美国独立战争的战斗檄文，它发表后，内战变成了独立革命，潘恩是当之无愧的美国"革命之父"。

最后，赶走英国总督、民族独立后，不应当沿袭英国式的君主立宪政体，而应当建立一个共和国。君主制是一切恶的来源，君主制是违反天意的，北美的王应当是宪章和法律。

《常识》对在大英帝国的威胁下摇摆不定的北美殖民地来说，可谓字字珠玑。华盛顿读完后说：它"在很多人心里，包括我自己在内，产生了一种极大的变化"。一家英文报纸说："《常识》无人不读，凡读它的人都改变了态度，哪怕一小时前他还是一个强烈反对独立思想的人。"《常识》流传之广是超乎想象的。当时北美不足200万人，该书销售四五十万册，所以成年人几乎人手一册。华盛顿率领的士兵背囊中，除了弹药、口粮外，几乎都有一本读得皱巴巴的《常识》。

1776年7月4日，杰弗逊起草的《独立宣言》宣布美利坚合众国从此脱离英国独立。"美利坚合众国"（the United States of America）的名字来自潘恩，杰弗逊坦承引用了《常识》，重复了其中的原则，并"引以为荣"。

在战争中，美军一度士气低落，纪律溃坏，几至瓦解。潘恩临危受命，应华盛顿之约再次拿起了他的笔，在行军途中垫着膝盖写下了一篇篇战斗檄文。"这是磨炼人的灵魂的时候，能共享安乐而不可共患难的人，在这场危机中将在为国服务中退缩，但现在能够抗住的人，应该受到男男女女的热爱和感谢。暴政同地狱一样是不容易征服的，但我们可以此安慰自己：斗争越艰苦，得来的胜利越光荣；得来的胜利越便宜，赢得的尊敬就越小。"华盛顿下令：集合全体官兵，向他们宣读这篇文章。

四处树敌的潘恩

抛头颅洒热血的革命家一般都做不好政治家，因为革命家一般都有天真未凿的率真，不然哪儿来的一腔热血？但是革命之后，从不轻易放弃发表自己的见解，常常会招致灾难。从进入独立后的美国政府任职之后，潘恩的人生开始逆转。

1777年，潘思被任命为大陆会议外交事务委员会秘书，1778年，他在报纸上公开揭露美国驻法商务代表塞拉斯·迪安等利用法国援助假公济私的行径。由于牵涉大面积当权人物，潘恩遭到排挤和公开打压。1779年，法国驻北美大使递交抗议书，说潘恩暴露了法国的秘密，要求大陆会议"对目前的状况采取适当的措施"。1779年，潘恩被迫辞职，他在辞呈中悲愤地说：他不是泄密，只是不愿渎职。

　　在美国待不下去，他回到了英国。法国大革命后，英国人热情讴歌，其中包括埃德蒙·伯克，潘恩的挚友。但是随着大革命的发展，习惯了改良主义的英国绅士们感到震惊不已。1791年，伯克发表了《法国革命感言录》攻击法国大革命，而作为革命家的潘恩，毫不犹豫地奋起迎战，他在伦敦激烈抨击伯克，批判英国政体，向法国人介绍美国的共和政体。

　　潘恩的影响力和激烈的言辞，震动了英法两国的媒体，他在法国社会引起的反响，堪比当年《常识》在美洲引起的影响。罗伯斯庇尔热情地赞颂他，1792年法国议会授予他荣誉国籍，加莱选他做议员，还专门派人去英国通知这位外国人已光荣当选。潘恩公然批判英国政体，且影响巨大，这激怒了英国的皮特内阁。1792年，英国政府指控潘恩犯煽动叛乱罪。美国回不去，潘恩只好流亡法国。潘恩在法国受到了英雄的礼遇，且被选为起草新宪法的九人小组之一。

　　潘恩对法国革命产生了巨大的影响，但和雅各宾派隔阂很大。罗伯斯庇尔一开始误会了潘恩，以为他也是个"斗士"，但很快大失所望。潘恩对路易十六的审判态度也激怒了雅各宾派。潘恩说：人们反对的应该是传统，而不是任何个人；法国大革命的可贵之处不在于和一个国王作对，而是和产生国王的制度作战。他公开反对处死国王。雅各宾派向来是不宽容的，执政后立刻删除了潘恩在宪法中的思想，并把他投进了监狱。而此时的英国，则已经开除了潘恩的国籍。于是他想求助于华盛顿，但曾经的朋友却没有伸出援助之手。

他在狱中写了《理性时代》，发表自己的宗教见解，表达自己以理性为基础的自然神论。这本书后来得罪了整个宗教界。

1794年，经过美国驻法大使门罗的四处奔走，潘恩终于获释，并在门罗夫妇的照料下恢复了健康。之后拿破仑曾访问过他。1797年秋天，拿破仑告诉潘恩：他枕头下面有他一本书，每晚睡前必读。他也曾宴请过潘恩，席间他说："世界上每一座城市都应为潘恩树立一座金质雕像。"但在拿破仑执政后，两人的关系却迅速冷却下来，因为潘恩厌弃一切类型的个人独裁，拒绝与他合作。

1802年，总统杰弗逊请潘恩回到美国。那本《理性时代》终于起了作用，正在建立民族宗教的美国，是容不得这些见解的。要知道，美国的超验主义自然神论大师爱默生要等到1803年才出世，他提前了半个世纪。天才往往都有悲惨的结局。杰弗逊为了避嫌，开始回避潘恩，甚至拒绝给他一官半职。本杰明·罗什也拒绝和潘恩有任何来往。邻居围攻潘恩，马车不愿载他，来往车辆故意溅他一身泥。

潘恩把那个年头能得罪的当权人物都得罪光了。在他那个时代，没有一个人像他一样热爱美国，但最排斥他的正是美国人民，没有一个人像他一样虔诚，放弃他的正是教会。背叛他的人，无论是英国的伯克，法国的罗伯斯庇尔、拿破仑，还是美国的华盛顿、杰弗逊、罗什，都曾经是他的战友，不久前还是他的同志，转身就不理他，甚至迫害他。

潘恩是一个革命家，革命家都是理想主义者，而天真的理想主义者不为他的时代所理解和接受，也在情理之中。没有圆熟的政治天赋，没有心机谋略，倒不是缺点，心底干净不是缺点，只是他激进的主张距离现世越来越遥远。他完成自己的使命后，就该归于历史了。作为美国革命史中最激进的政治理论家，潘恩很适用舍伍德·安德森评价小镇中的"畸人"的话，他是"秋天枝头弃摘的果子，其甘美只有少数人懂得品尝"。

序 言
（再版）

也许本书所述思想**暂时**不足以流行并获得普遍认可。只要长期习惯了一件**错误的**事就不会去质疑，以至于它表面看起来就是**正确的**，一旦出现反对声音就会激起捍卫传统的可怕呼声。但反动的呼号很快就会过去，时间比逻辑更有说服力。

当权力长期暴力滥用，人们就会质疑这种权力是否合法（当然，一旦受害者被逼到奋身质疑的地步，一些始料未及的事情也会牵连其中）。因为英格兰国王认为**自己有权利**支持**议会**①**的权利**，这片土地②上的善良人民就遭受了严酷的双重压迫，于是他们就拥有了不容置疑的权利，质疑国王和议会的借口，同样有权利反对两者对权利的僭越。

---

① 英国议会。
② 北美大陆。

笔者在书中极力避免谈论关于我们个人方面的事情，所以没有针对个人的赞美或谴责。智者和有尊严的人无需一本小册子来打动，而不明智和不友好的人会继续固执已见，只有更多的伤害才能使其疼醒。

美洲的事业在很大程度上是全人类的事业，一直在发生并将继续发生很多事情，具有普遍意义而非地方性意义，这些事情触到了所有爱人之人的原则，这些事件唤醒了人们的情感。有人企图用火和剑使一片土地沦为废墟，向全人类的天赋权利宣战，企图把捍卫者从地球表面消灭干净。所有接受了自然①赐予的情感能力②的人都在密切关注，而其中一个超越党派纠纷的人就是**作者**③。

---

① Nature在基督教体系中，相当于上帝旨意的落实和外化。所以它有很多层意思，第一层是"造物"，第二层是"上帝的旨意"，第三层是"不可抗拒的规律"，所以托马斯·潘恩口中的nature，在下文中我们根据语境还可能会翻译成"天道""造化"等。在某些方面，nature有些类似于老子的"道"。
② 类似于老子所谓"德"。
③ 这里是个双关语，因为造物主常被比喻为万物的"作者"。而某些作家常把自己比作自己作品的上帝（比如亨利·菲尔丁之于《汤姆·琼斯》），电影或电视的"总编剧"的英文就是creator（造物主）。

另外，新版的发表略微延迟，因为我一直在关注（觉得可能有必要关注）任何反对独立原则的企图，但目前仍未出现反对意见。既然对公众有个交代的截止时间已经过了，现在只能假定没人会反对了。大家完全没有必要知道本书的作者是谁[1]，因为值得关注的是**主旨本身**而不是**人**。但仍有必要指出，他和任何党派都没有任何瓜葛，也没有受到任何官方或个人的影响，他只遵循理性和原则。

费城[2]，1776年2月14日[3]

---

① 初版发表时作者署名为"一个英国人"。
② 1790年后，华盛顿建市之前，这是美国的首府。
③ 本书初版于1776年1月。

第一章

概论政府的起源和目的
&
简评英格兰政体

　　有些作家把社会和政府混为一谈，认为两者没有或很少有区别。但实际上它们不仅不是一回事，而且从根本起源上就不一样。社会由我们的需要产生，而政府则由我们的邪恶而来。前者通过凝聚我们的情感**积极**促进我们的幸福，后者则制止我们的恶行**消极**地增进我们的幸福。一个鼓励互动，另一个制造界线。前者是奖励者，后者则是惩罚者。

　　任何状态的社会都是祝福，但政府呢？即使最好的政府也只是一个必要的诅咒，最坏的政府则是无法忍受的祸害，因为当我们受苦，遭受政府造成的、只有无政府国家中才会存在的不幸，想到正是自己养活了使我们受苦的机构，我们就会感到分外痛心。政府就像衣服，标志着纯真的丧失①；国

―――――――――
① 亚当和夏娃失去纯真后，发现自己赤身裸体，才开始寻找东西遮挡身体。

王的宫殿就建筑在伊甸园亭榭的废墟上。假如良心的冲动是清澈的，所有人都无法抗拒地遵守，人就不需要其他立法者了，但事实并非如此。人们发现有必要放弃一部分财产，买到一种方法来保护其余财产；这样做是因为一种智慧，一切世事都教会了他们在两害面前要取其轻。所以，安全是政府的真正目的和结果，所以无可辩驳的推论就是，我们认为哪种形式最能保证我们的安全，代价最小，受益最大，其他所有人也会愿意接受。

为了清晰而准确地把握政府的目的和结果，我们可以假设有几个人在地球上某个与世隔绝的偏僻角落住了下来。他们可以代表任何一块土地的第一批移民，或世界上的第一批移民。在这种自然的自由状态下，他们首先会想到社会，千百种动机都会使其趋向于社会。一个人的力量实在无法满足自己的各种需要，而他的心灵也扛不住太久的孤独，所以很快他便被迫寻求他人的帮助和安慰，而对方也有同样的需要。四五个人联合起来，就能在荒野中建起一个还算过得去的住所。而单个人则可能劳碌一生亦无所获，也许他砍倒树后搬不动，或能搬动但竖不起来，同时饥饿会迫使他放下工作……各种不同的匮乏都需要他进行不同的满足。疾病，甚至一件小小的不幸，都意味着死亡，因为虽然它们并不致命，但都会使他无法生活，虽然没有死，他已经陷入了可以叫作"萎缩"的状态。

所以，客观需要就像引力一样把新来的移民迅速地组成社会。互相给予的幸福随之而来，只要人们保持完全真诚相待，就不会需要法律和政府的约束。但是，只有老天不会被恶侵蚀①，所以注定会发生这种情况：他们在克服移民初期遭遇的困难（这些困难把他们团结在一份共同的事业中）后，现在逐渐淡忘自己的责任和对彼此的情谊。这种淡忘会导致必须建立某种形式的政府，以弥补精神美德的缺陷。

选一棵树就能供他们开议会用，全体移民可以聚集在树荫下，讨论公共问题。他们制定的第一批法律只能叫作约定，

---

① 基督教认为，人人生而有堕落的倾向。这是人性本恶论的基础。魔鬼虎视眈眈地准备吞噬任何人，尤其那些有条件的人，比如拥有财富、权力、名誉的人。

无法用任何刑罚保证，除了公众的鄙视。在这第一次会议中，每个人都有占一席位的自然权利。

但随着聚居地的扩大，公共事业也会增加，而成员间的距离也在扩大，当初每次大家都聚在一起，现在就太不方便了。那时人数还很少，住处很近，公众事业都是小事，也不多，掰着手指头就能数清。这时就需要他们授权，从全体成员中选出一定的人员来专门管理立法工作，被选的人应该关心那些把他们选出来的人所关心的事，应当像全体成员亲自出席时一样行动。如果聚居地继续发展，就必须增加代表名额，且要兼顾聚居地每个部分的利益，所以最好把整个聚居地适当分成若干部分，每一部分派出一定人数。而且要保证，代表们绝对不能形成与选民无干的利益，为了审慎起见，最好常常举行选举。通过这种方式，代表们会在几个月后回归并混杂于人群，所以在位时会谨慎地考虑到权杖并不是自己的，这就保证了他们对公众的忠诚。这种频繁的换届会使社会的各个部分休戚相关，各部分自然会互相支持。政府的力量和民众的幸福正是基于这一点。找个人叫他国王，是毫无价值的。

　　这就是政府的起源和兴起。政府即精神美德无力管理世界时的必要模式，这也是政府的目的和结果，即自由与安全。即使跳梁的表演迷乱了我们的眼睛，或者声音欺骗了我们的耳朵，即使执念扭曲了我们的意志意愿，或者利益迷住了我们的心智，自然和理性的声音仍会简单地说：这①是对的。

　　我从无法人为推翻的自然法则中推出政体的概念。这条自然法则就是：一件事越简单就越不容易乱，即使乱了也容易恢复。根据这个箴言，我想对大肆吹嘘英格兰政体的人说两句。刚刚脱离黑暗的附庸时代时，它是高贵的，我同意这一点；当暴政蹂躏世界时，即使脱离一点点也是光荣的救赎。②但这种政体是有缺陷的、不稳定的，无法产生它貌似预示的结果，这很容易证明。

---

① 这＝没有国王。
② 指英国脱离罗马教廷。

专制政府是人性的耻辱，但拥有这个优点：它们简单。如果人民受苦，就知道苦难源自何处，也知道补救的方法，不会有一堆让人茫然不知所措的病因和药方。但英国政体极其复杂，可能整个国家受苦多年也无法弄清到底哪儿出了问题，众说纷纭，每个政治医生都会开出一个不同的药方。

我知道要克服地域式或长期存在的偏见是困难的，但如果不花点儿精力仔细剖析英国政体的各个组成部分，就无法看出它只是两种古代暴政的渣滓，新掺了一点儿共和因素。

第一，它有国王，君主暴政的残余。

第二，它有上议院①，贵族暴政的残余。

第三，它有下议院，英格兰的自由指望着他们的美德，这是新掺的共和因素。

_____

① 又称元老院，由贵族组成。

前两种是世袭的，与人民隔绝，所以从体制角度讲，无益于国家的自由。

有人说英国政体是三种力量的凝聚，互生牵制之效。这话真可笑，它毫无意义，且完全自相矛盾。

有人说下议院制约国王，这有两个假定条件：

第一，如果无人监管，国王是无法信任的，或换句话说，对绝对权力的渴望是君主政体的固有弊病。

第二，为此而设的下议院议员必须比国王贤明，更值得信赖。

这个政体授权下议院制约国王，可以否决他的预算，同时又授权国王制约下议院，可以否决它的其他议案。这样，这个政体就又假设国王比众议院更贤明，而它早已假设下议院比国王贤明。真是荒唐透顶！

　　君主政体中有极其可笑的东西，它先让一个人无法获得学识，然后授权他裁决那些需要最高理智的案件。国王的地位使其不知世事，但他又需要通晓一切才能履行职责。所以，不同的方面畸形地对立和抵消，证明其整体性质是荒唐无用的。

　　有些作家这样解释英国政体。他们说：国王是一端，人民是另一端；上议院代表国王，下议院代表人民。但这样一来，议会自己就分裂成两个对立的东西了。虽然那话文采斐然，但一经推敲，就显得模棱两可、毫无用处了。而且这种情况很常见，字词组成了最漂亮的语句，描述不可能存在的事物或太费解所以无法描述的事物，但那也只能是一堆字词、一阵声响，虽然悦耳，仔细思考却没有什么意义。那个漂亮的解释还包含一个内在的问题，即**为什么国王拥有一种人民不敢信任又总有义务制约的权力？**这种权力绝不会赋予一个智慧的民族，任何**需要外来牵制的权力**都不是来自上帝，但宪法却有条文规定要存在这样的权力。

　　但法律和它的任务并不匹配。^①法律手段不能也无法达成目的，所以整件事就成了法律在说"我不行"。大砝码总能压起较轻的那头，机器的所有齿轮都由一个齿轮推动，我们只需知道机制中哪个权力是最有力的，那个权力拥有的叫统治权。虽然其他权力（或部分其他权力）可以妨碍（或所谓牵制）它的运转速度，但只要无法使其停止，一切就都是无用功，第一动力终将为所欲为，而提高速度只是时间的问题。

　　王权是统治英国政体的那一部分，这不必多说。他只靠封爵和赐予爵位年金获得全部权力，这是不言自明的。所以，虽然我们^②足够聪明关闭了专制君主政体的大门，但同时十分愚蠢地让国王掌管了钥匙。

　　英国人喜欢他们由国王、贵族上议院和下议院组成的政府，固执的狭隘思想一半来自民族自豪，一半来自理性，但

---

① 根据本段下文可知，这句话的意思是：国王比法律大，那么法律规定国王的权力，就成了一件越权的事情。
② 潘恩发表本书时署名"一个英国人"，所以"我们"指"英国人"。此时的北美是英国殖民地，所以美洲人名义上都是英国人。

前者可能更多。在英国，个人无疑要比在其他国家更安全一些，但英王的圣旨跟法皇一样都是国家法律，区别只是，英王不直接下令而是把圣旨用议会法案的恐怖形式传达给人民。查理一世①的命运只是使国王们更加狡猾，而非更加公正。

所以，支持某种结构或形式的政府的执念与民族自大主义，我们暂且不谈，简单的真理是：**英王之所以不像土耳其国王那样暴虐，完全是因为人民的素质，而不是政府的体制。**

此时很有必要探讨英国政府形式在体制方面的错误。如果不摆脱某种执念爱好的影响，我们就无法公正地看待他人；同理，当我们被顽固的偏见束缚时，也无法公正地对待自己。一个男人如果眷恋妓女，就不配选择或判断妻子；对腐朽政体怀着好感的执念，我们就不能识别健全的政体。

---

① 被斩首的英国国王。

第二章

论君主政体与世袭

　　在万物的秩序中，人类本来是平等的。但这种平等被后来的事情破坏了，贫富差别可能是一大原因，不必求助于压迫、贪婪之类刺耳、难听的字眼。压迫往往是财富的**结果**，而很少是或从不是致富的手段。贪婪虽然会保证一个人不至于陷入赤贫，但一般会让人变得懦弱而无法致富。

　　但还有一种更大的差别，不能用纯自然或宗教的原因来解释，即人竟然要分为**国王**和**臣民**。自然中分有雌雄，上苍区分善恶。但为什么会有一类人降生时就高居他人之上，俨然一个新的物种。这倒是值得研究研究，看看他们到底给人类带来了幸福还是苦难。

　　根据圣经记载的历史来看，世界上一开始是没有王的，没有王的结果就是没有战争，正是国王的傲慢使人类陷入混乱。没有王的荷兰，一百年来享受的和平比欧洲任何君主政体的国家都多。①古人的情况也支持这种说法，最初的部落长老们过着恬静、悠然的田园生活，当犹太人有了王之后这种幸福就消失了。②

由国王统治的政府形式是异教徒发明的，后来以色列的子孙才复制了这个习惯。这是魔鬼为了鼓励偶像崇拜③而发明的最得意的创造。异教徒把死去的国王敬拜为神，而基督教世界则改进了方案，敬拜活着的国王。用"圣上"称呼一只耀武扬威但顷刻即将化为尘土的蠕虫，是何等的渎神之罪啊！

一个人的位置远高于他人，这违背了平等权利原则这条

---

① 1648年，尼德兰联邦正式从西班牙帝国中独立出来，成为荷兰共和国。
② 犹太人的第一个王是扫罗，《圣经·撒母耳记上》中，以色列人求立王，撒母耳转告上帝的话："管辖你们的王必这样行：他必派你们的儿子为他赶车、跟马、奔走在车前……那时，你们必因所选的王哀求耶和华，耶和华却不应允你们。"
③ 十诫第一诫是"除我之外不可有他神"，第二诫实际上是第一诫的延伸。总之，最大的罪就是偶像崇拜。

天理，也无法以圣经的权威进行辩护，因为根据基甸①和先知撒母耳所述，万能的上帝的意志明显是反对由王统治政府的。圣经中反对君主的部分，在君主国家被巧妙地掩饰了，但无疑值得那些尚待组建政府的国家的注意。王庭援引圣经教义的恺撒的归恺撒②，但教义根本就不支持君主政府，因为当时犹太人没有自己的王，而是沦为罗马人的附庸。

从摩西描述创世起，到犹太人在对国家的幻想中求立王，三千年就过去了。在立王以前，他们的管理形式（除了万能上帝亲自插手的特殊情况外）是一种共和体制，由一位士师和各部落长老管理。他们没有王，他们认为，除万军之王耶和华外，称任何存在为王都是罪恶。当人认真思考对君主之类的人进行的偶像崇拜，就不会惊讶于万能的上帝（他永远都忌讳自己的荣耀为人所夺）为什么要反对这种形式的政府，它悍然染指上天的权力。

_____

①《旧约·士师记》中的人物。基甸从敌人手上拯救了以色列人，于是以色列人希望基甸做王。但基甸说："我不管理你们，我的儿子也不管理你们，唯有耶和华管理你们。"
②《新约·马可福音》中，有人试探基督，问是否该给恺撒纳税，基督便说："恺撒的归恺撒，上帝的归上帝。"

君主制在圣经中被列为犹太人的一宗罪，他们因此受到诅咒，早晚受罚。这段历史值得注意。

以色列的子民被米甸人压迫，基甸带着一小支军队①进攻他们，并在上帝的帮助下得胜。犹太人得胜后十分高兴，将其归功于基甸的雄才大略，要立他为王，说：**愿你治理我们，你的儿子孙子也治理我们。**这是最大的诱惑了，不只是王位，而且可以传给后代，但基甸的灵魂是虔诚的，他回答说：**我不管理你们，我的儿子也不管理你们，唯有耶和华管理你们。**这话说得最清楚了，基甸并非拒绝荣耀，而是否认他们有赐予荣耀的权利，他也没有编出一套官话婉谢，而是用先知特有的坚定语气，指责他们背叛自己真正的主宰，即天上的王。

此后约130年，他们又犯了同样的错误。犹太人要遵循异教的偶像崇拜的风俗，渴望的程度无以言表，他们抓住撒母耳的两个儿子在任上的不端行为，吵闹着冲到撒母耳面前说：

---

① 300人。

看啊，你年纪老了，你的儿子又不行你的道。现在请你为我们立一个王治理我们，像列国一样。在这里，我们不会看不出他们的邪恶用心，即，他们希望像那些异教国家一样，而在异教国度荣耀被归于完全不配得到它的人。**撒母耳不喜悦他们说"立一个王治理我们"，他就向耶和华祷告。耶和华对撒母耳说："百姓向你说的一切话，你只管依从。因为他们不是厌弃你，乃是厌弃我，不要我做他们的王。自从我领他们出埃及到如今，他们常常离弃我，侍奉别神。现在他们向你所行的，是照他们素来所行的。故此，你要依从他们的话，只是当警戒他们，告诉他们将来那王怎样管辖他们。"**[①]也就是说，以色列人不是想要一个个体做王，而是急于模仿世上他国的普遍做法，要一个王。时过境迁，现在的方式不同了但性质没有改变。**撒母耳将耶和华一切的话转告求他立王的百姓。他说："管辖你们的王必用这样的方式：他必派你们的儿子为他驾车，赶马，在他的战车前奔跑**（这种描述符合现在强征兵丁的方式）。**他要为自己立千夫长、五十夫长；耕种**

---

① 《旧约·撒母耳记》。

他的田地，收割他的庄稼；打造他的兵器和车上的器械。**必取你们的女儿为他制造香膏，做饭烤饼**（这描述了国王的奢侈浪费和压迫手段）；**也必取你们最好的田地、葡萄园、橄榄园，赐给他的臣仆。你们的粮食和葡萄园所出的，他必取十分之一给他的太监和臣仆**（从中我们可以看到受贿、腐败、徇私是国王们一贯的恶行）；**又必取你们的仆人婢女、健壮的少年人和你们的驴，供他的差役。你们的羊群，他必取十分之一，你们也必做他的仆人。那时，你们必因所选的王哀求耶和华，耶和华却不应允你们。**"最后这句说明了君主制续存的原因。自古以来屈指可数的明君，其德行也不足以僭越"王"这一名号，也不能抹除它的原罪。圣经对大卫的赞颂，并不是赞颂履行王的职责的大卫，而是夸赞他是一个遵从上帝心意的人。**百姓却不肯听撒母耳的话，说："不！我们一定要一个王治理我们，使我们像列国一样，有王治理我们，率领我们，为我们争战。"**撒母耳继续和他们理论，结果没用；他把他们的忘恩负义放在他们面前，结果都是白费；看到他们愚蠢且固执，他喊道：**我求告耶和华，他必打雷降雨，**（因为正是收麦的季节，所以这是一种惩罚）**让你们知道并且看**

出，你们为自己求立王的事在耶和华眼前是犯大罪了。于是撒母耳求告耶和华，耶和华就在这日打雷降雨，众百姓就非常惧怕耶和华和撒母耳。众民对撒母耳说："求你为仆人们祷告耶和华你的神，免得我们死亡，因为我们求立王的事，正是罪上加罪了。"圣经的这几个部分都是直接而肯定的，不容他解。只要这段圣经不是伪造的，那么万能的上帝就是在反对君主制。人们有充分的理由相信，在教皇制①的国家里，国王和神职人员都用尽权术不让大众了解这些经文，因为君主制无一例外都是教皇制的统治。

但在君主制的恶之外，还要加上世袭制的恶。前者是人类的堕落和自我的贬低，而后者却被视为一种权利，这样骗小孩都算侮辱他们的智商。因为人人而平等，所以没有**任何人仅凭出身**就有权让自己的家族永远高于其他家族，虽然某些人也许值得同时代人在**某种**程度上尊敬，他的后代却可能

---

① 英王亨利八世脱离罗马教廷，建立英国国教，自命最高宗教首领，也就是"英国的教皇"。在新教中一般认为，除了耶稣基督之外没有第二个首领。所以，潘恩认为英国也是教皇制的国家，只不过不受罗马教廷的制约。

根本没有资格继承。一个最强有力且明显的事情可以证明国王的世袭权是荒唐的，即，天道反对它，否则它就不会这样经常地把笨驴权当雄狮①，遗人笑柄了。

其次，第一代可以拥有被授予的社会荣誉，但荣誉的授予者没有权力代替子孙放弃权利。人们可以说"我们选你做**我们的王**"，但他们不能说"你的子孙和子孙的子孙可以永远统治**我们的**子孙和我们子孙的子孙"，这明显是侵犯了后代的权利，因为这可能把子孙置于一个恶棍或蠢货的统治之下，所以这个契约是愚蠢、不公平、天理不容的。贤达人士对世袭权多持暗自蔑视的态度，但它是一种一旦确立就很难纠正的恶。很多人因恐惧而服从，有些人是出于迷信，而强势阶级则和国王联合起来一起抢劫其他人。

人们普遍假设，世上的皇族都有光荣的祖先，但当我们

①《伊索寓言》中有个故事是这样的。有头驴发现一张狮子皮，就披起它来招摇，所有的人和动物都吓跑了。驴子感到很得意，就大声嘶叫，结果他的主人跑过来打了它一顿。不久，一只狐狸跑过来说："啊，你一张嘴我就知道你是驴。"英王应当是一头雄狮，国徽上也刻着狮子，但潘恩讽刺他们为蠢驴。由此可以看出，潘恩是一个非常激进的人，或者说很偏激。

扯掉古代的遮羞布，追溯他们最初的发迹，更可能发现的是，其祖先不过是某个强盗团伙的贼魁，因为杀人越货时更加野蛮或因为比别人更加诡诈所以赢得了盗贼头头的称号。而当他们权力渐盛，地盘扩大，就恐吓手无寸铁的平头百姓按时贡献财物购买安全。但选他当头儿的人们绝对不想把世袭权交给他的子孙，因为这样做就永远放弃了自己的权利，这和他们①声称的生活原则不符，也就是不受束缚的自由原则。所以一开始，君主世袭制并不是理所当然的，只是一种临时的补充，但那个时代几乎或根本没有文字记录留存，而口耳相传的历史则充满了虚构的故事，所以隔几代之后就很容易编出一些迷信故事，就像异教徒编的那些鬼话一样，适时地大肆传播，把世袭权灌进百姓的喉咙。或许头领死亡后要选新头领时的骚乱威胁（或骚乱威胁的可能，因为选强盗头子不可能很文明），让许多人第一次赞同世袭的主张。它就这样成了，并成了传统，所以，最初的权宜之计后来就被硬说成了一种权利。

① 海盗。

自从英格兰被征服，^①出的明君是有数的那么几个，所以它一直在大量昏君的统治下呻吟。智者绝对不会说在威廉一世的统治下享有权利是件光荣的事。一个法国浑蛋带了一帮武装土匪登陆，未经本地人民同意强行自立英格兰国王，说白了这流氓祖先还真够贱的，显然没什么神圣意味。但我们无须多费时间揭露世袭权的荒唐了，如果有谁心智弱到竟然相信它，那就让他蠢蠢地崇拜那头雄狮兼蠢驴吧，随便。我不会效仿他们的卑贱，也不会妨碍他们的虔诚。

但我倒很想问一下，他们认为国王最早是怎么产生的？这个问题只可能有三个答案，不是天命就是选举，或者篡政。如果第一任国王由上天拣选，接下来就有了先例，所以王位不能世袭。扫罗^②因天命为王，但王位不世袭，而且从始至终都没有痕迹，说明他有世袭的打算。如果某国的第一任王是选举出来的，同样也给后来者立了先例，也

① 1066年，征服者威廉征服英格兰，他是诺曼底公爵，而诺曼底公爵是一个法国爵位称号。
② 以色列第一任王，由上帝拣选，撒母耳膏立，后远离上帝。第二位王是大卫王。

得选举。如果第一批选民剥夺子孙未来的一切权利，不是
选一个王而是选一个永远的王族，那么除了人类的自由意
志都断送于亚当之手这一原罪教义外，整部圣经和所有神
学中都没有解释。和亚当的原罪一比较（不可能有别的对
照），世袭是没有什么荣耀在里面的。人类因亚当而获罪，
因当初的投票者而臣服；因前者而受制于撒旦，因后者而
受制于国王；因前者丧失了纯洁，因后者丧失了自我掌控
权。既然两者都使我们无法重获某种权利，回到曾经的状
态，无疑可以推出，世袭和原罪是类似的。多么丢脸的并
列！多么可耻的连接！但这是实打实的，最高明的雄辩家
也找不到更恰当的对比了。

　　说到篡政，没有人会愿意为它辩护。而征服者威廉是个
篡政者①，这是不容置疑的事实。明摆着的事实是，英王的祖
先真是令人不忍直视啊。

_____

① 征服者威廉本为法国诺曼底公爵。英王忏悔者爱德华死后无嗣，贵族哈罗德被
立。威廉借口爱德华生前曾许以王位，渡海侵入英国，击毙哈罗德，自立为英王。

但让人担心的并不是世袭权的荒谬，而是它带来的恶。如果它保证提供一群善良的明君，那倒可以算获得了神权的特许，但实际上它给**愚蠢的、邪恶的和下流的**人开了门，所以本身就带着压迫的性质。自知生来就是要做王统治他人的人，很快就会变得傲慢。由于和其他人不同，他们从小就被妄自尊大毒害了心灵。他们生活于其中的小世界，和大世界有显著的不同，所以很少有机会认识世界的真正可爱，而当他们继承了统治权，常常是最无知的，一无所用，比整个疆土内的任何人都差劲。

世袭自带的另一种恶是，王座常由一个年龄极小的未成年人占据，其间以国王作掩护的实权人物就有一切机会和诱惑去背叛人们对他的信任。当老国王年老体衰，风烛残年时，也会发生同样的国家灾难。在两种情况下，民众都沦为各种恶棍的牺牲品，他们可以成功地耍一套符合他们那个年龄段的勾当。

世袭制的支持者们提出过的貌似最言之成理的理由就是，

它保全国家使其不发生内战。假如这是真的，那倒很有分量，但实际上它是骗人的、最不要脸的谎言。英格兰的整个历史都否认它的真实性。自从英格兰被征服，一共有30个国王和两个幼王统治这个动乱的王国，其间发生过8次以上内战和19次叛乱（包括光荣革命在内）。所以，它并未带来和平，而是有损和平。那个理由仿佛有根有据，实际上自己就摧毁了自己的根据。

　　兰开斯特家族和约克家族之间争夺王位继承权的斗争，使英格兰多年沦为流血的战场。①亨利和爱德华激烈地打过12次战役，小冲突和围城战不计在内。亨利两次为爱德华所掳，爱德华也被抓住过。当争端只是个人私事，战争的命运和人民的脾气就不确定了，所以亨利从监狱回到王宫，胜了，而爱德华则被迫从王宫逃往外国。但突变的脾气很难持久，亨利又被赶下王位，爱德华被召回来继任。议会总是在倒向力量更强大的一边。

────────────

① 英王爱德华三世的两支后裔兰开斯特家族和约克家族为了争夺英格兰王位挑起内战，因为前一家以红玫瑰为族徽，后一家以白玫瑰为族徽，所以称为"玫瑰战争"。

从亨利六世当政时就开始打了，直到亨利七世统一王室各家族时还没完全打完，其间共67年，即从1422年起至1489年。[①]

总之，君主制和世袭制使整个世界（不是某一个王国）陷于血泊和废墟之中。这是上帝之言所反对的管理形式，所以流血在所难免。

如果研究一下国王都干些什么，我们就会发现，有些国家的国王无事可做，他们熬完了对自己没益处、对国家没好处的一生之后，就会让出舞台，让王储步过同样虚度的一生。在君主专制的国家，所有的内政和军事重担都置于国王一身。以色列的子孙求立王时曾请求，希望"有王治理我们，率领我们，为我们争战"。但在英国这样的国家里，国王既非士师，又非将军，着实让人很为难，不知道他到底是**干什么工作的**。

---

① 兰开斯特家族的亨利七世1485 年即位，娶约克家族的伊丽沙白为后，两个家族的联姻基本结束了玫瑰战争。关于玫瑰战争的开始年份，现在普遍接受的说法是1455年，而不是1422年。

　　任何政府越接近共和制，需要国王做的事就越少。要给英国政府想一个适当的叫法多少有些困难。威廉·梅瑞迪斯爵士把它叫共和国，但目前这种状态不配这个名称，因为国王有权任意安排所有官员，所以王冠有腐蚀力。实际上国王独揽了权力，侵蚀了下议院（体制中的共和部分）的美德，所以英国政府和法国、西班牙是几乎一模一样的君主制。人们如果不理解名称的真正含义，是不配使用的。英国人引为骄傲的不应当是其政体中的君主部分，而应当是其共和部分，也就是从全体民众中选出来的下议院。我们很容易明白，当共和的美德失效，奴役便接踵而至。英国政体之所以是病态的，除了王冠毒害共和、国王裹挟下议院外还有别的解释吗？

　　在英格兰，国王能做的事只有挑起战争和送送官位，说白了，结果只能使国家贫穷、人心背离。求着你买一个职位，买到后给你80万镑的年金，真是笔好买卖！一个诚实的人对社会的价值更大吧，在上帝的眼里，从古至今加冕的恶棍有什么价值可言。

第三章

对美洲^① 当下情况的思考

---

① 这里的美洲指北美洲。

在接下来的若干页中，我只提供简单的事实、直白的论证以及常识。我想请读者提前准备好，也不是别的什么，我只请你摆脱偏见和成见，把一切困难都交给理智和情感独自判断，这样，你就能拥有（或毋宁说是不失去）真正的人类性格，不受当下限制，放眼未来。

关于英格兰和美洲之间的斗争问题，已经出版过大量书籍。各阶层的人带着不同的动机和目的参加了论战①。但是一

---

① 指美洲内部的意见分歧。论战以"莱克星顿的枪声"为转折点分为两部分。之前的主题是，如何做好英国的附属，之后的主题是，该独立还是该议和。本书作就之时，正是美洲人在独立和议和之间犹豫不决的时候。

现在看来，那些意见分歧是很荒唐的，但是殖民地的人对英国是有眷恋的，很多人认为英国是自己的故乡，到美洲来只不过是做点儿生意发点儿财好回家。本书的历史价值就在于，它使美洲坚定了在政治上独立的决心。

但那种故国情结在美国建国后一百多年都没有消失，变成了后来的"文化故乡情结"。当时的美国被认为是文化的沙漠，美国人都是暴发户、土包子，让人瞧不起。诸多大文豪比如欧文、霍桑都认为自己是文化上的英国人，用美国的材料承载英国的主题。而像庞德、海明威等，则旅居欧洲。大文豪艾略特在英国文学史和美国文学史上都有其名，因为他后来加入了英国籍。

切都是徒劳，现在论战早已过时，①武力已经成为决定英美之间斗争的最终因素。诉诸武力是英王的选择，而美洲大陆已经接受了挑战。

据报道，已故的佩勒姆先生②（一个能干的大臣，虽然也有自己的过错）因为某些措施治标不治本而被下议院质疑，他回答说："我愿倾尽一生维持现状。"如果殖民地的人民在目前的斗争中抱着这种致命的懦弱想法，将来的子孙会以他们祖先的名字为耻的。

太阳从未照耀过一份更高尚的事业。这不是涉及一城、一县、一州或一国的事业，而是涉及整整一个大陆，至少占地球可居住面积的八分之一。这不是一天、一年或一个年代③的事，实际上后代子孙也都牵涉到了斗争之中，并且时

---

① 潘恩认为，"莱克星顿的枪声"一发生，再在道理上争个长短就没有什么意义了。但是这时候的美洲内部还是分裂的，有人主张议和，有人主张独立。一个月后的大陆会议对是否宣布独立仍然犹豫不决。

② 亨利·佩勒姆，1694年9月—1754年3月，1743年—1754年为英国第三任首相。

③ 这里的年代指10年，如"19世纪70年代"。

间的尽头①也多多少少会受目前形势的影响。现在是大陆团结起来、播撒信念和荣誉的种子的时候。今天的一小点儿裂隙，都会像针尖刻在小橡树嫩皮上的名字，伤痕会随着树的生长而扩大，子子孙孙都能清晰地读到醒目的大字。

　　问题从论战转向武力，开启了新的政治纪元，新的思维方式已经产生。4月19日②以前，即撕破脸③以前的一切的计划、提议等都成了老皇历。那些东西当时是合适的，现在则成了无用的废品。当年论战双方提出的意见，最后归结到了同一点，即不脱离大不列颠。两派唯一的区别在于实施方法：一方建议展示力量④，一方提议诉诸友谊⑤。但到目前为止发生的事情是，前者完败，后者也不再有影响力。

---

① 在有些宗教中，比如佛教，时间是轮回的，是个圈。而在基督教体系中，时间是有始有终的，当基督再次临世，便是时间的终点。
② 1775年4月18日夜，英军从据点波士顿出动，企图夺取军需，武装起来的北美人民出来迎击英军，于4月19日在莱克星顿和康科德一带发生了战斗。这就是"莱克星顿的枪声"。
③ 潘恩认为这就算撕破脸了，但当时的美洲人并不都这样认为。
④ 比如拒绝和英国贸易，直到英国下议院撤销对美洲的法案。以失败告终，英王并不吃这一套。
⑤ 也就是在英国下议院游走斡旋，以求其撤销对美洲的恶法。

036

和解的好处已经被说过很多，和解就像美梦一样幻灭了，没带来一丝好处，所以我们理应考查一下主张的反面，考查一下殖民地因附属于大不列颠而遭受并将永远遭受的许多实质性伤害，根据自然法则和常识考查这种纽带和附庸关系，看看如果独立必须依靠什么，如果继续附属将失去什么。

我听有人主张说：美洲作为大不列颠的附属一直繁荣，所以为了美洲将来的福祉，同样的关系是必要的且将永远带来同样的繁荣。没有什么比这种论断更荒唐了。这还不如说，因为儿童都是吃奶长大的，所以他绝不能吃肉，或者说，我们一生的前20岁怎么过，后20岁也得那么过。我可以坦率地回击，假如美洲不和任何欧洲强国勾扯不清，它照样能够繁荣，说不准还能更繁荣，而这才比真理更真。美洲赖以兴盛的贸易商品都是生活必需品，只要欧洲人还有吃饭的传统，那就不会没有市场。

还有人说，英国保护过我们。不错，它是我们的宗主国，我也承认它保卫美洲时没有只花我们的钱，它也做了牺牲，但是，如果是为了做生意和统治的目的，即使是土耳其也会这么干。

　　啊，我们长期以来被历史性偏见所误导，又因为迷信牺牲了很多。我们胡吹受到大不列颠的保护，而不考虑它是为了**利益**而不是**情义**。它从未为了**我们的原因**保护我们不受**我们的敌人**的侵扰，而是为了**它自己的原因**去防御它自己的敌人。他们只是和英国有仇才迁怒我们并将一直**因为这个原因**是我们的敌人，我们没有**任何其他理由**和他们起冲突。如果英国放弃它对美洲的主权，或者美洲摆脱从属地位，那么，当法国、西班牙和英国打仗，我们也能和两国和平共处。汉诺威王朝①上次打仗带给我们的苦难应该警示我们不要和英国有什么牵扯。

　　最近议会②里有人主张：北美十三州除通过母国相连，彼此之间没有什么关系，也就是说，宾夕法尼亚、新泽西等所

---

① 当时的英国处于汉诺威王朝时期。
② 指英国下议院。

有州，都是通过英格兰建立起来的姊妹殖民地。这当然是转弯抹角地套近乎，但它也是树敌（如果我可以这么说）的最直接和唯一正确的方法。如果我们不是**大不列颠**的臣民，法国和西班牙可能从来不是且永远不是**我们美洲人**的敌人。

有人说英国是母国。那么它的作为就更可耻了。虎毒不食子，蛮族不伐亲。所以如果那个说法是对的，就是在指责它了。但这碰巧是错的，或者只是部分正确，而英王和他那伙寄生虫使用的**母国**或**故国**的字眼，含有卑鄙险恶的用心，他们企图利用我们老实的弱点灌输他高我低的偏见。欧洲才是美洲的母国，而不是英格兰。这个新世界为欧洲**各地**热爱公民和宗教自由的受迫害人士提供避难所。他们逃到这里，并不是逃离母亲温柔的拥抱，而是逃离凶残的怪物。英格兰亦然。把最初的移民赶出故乡使其浪迹天涯的暴政，不肯放过他们的子孙。

在地球上这片广阔地域，让我们忘记360英里（英格兰的长度）的小窄条吧，让我们在更大的范围里寻找友谊，和欧洲的每个基督徒保持兄弟情谊[①]，并为自己广阔的胸襟感到自豪。

　　研究一下个体在一步步认识世界的过程中，要经历多少步才能克服小地方的偏见，是很有趣的。英格兰一个镇就是一个堂区[②]，既然生于此，自然和本堂区的人联系最多（因为他们在很多方面休戚相关），并互称**街坊**以识别；如果他们在离家几英里外的镇子相遇，就会丢掉街道的小概念，互称**同镇人**；如果走出本郡，在别的郡相遇，他们就会忘掉街道和城镇的小区域，互称**同乡**，即**来自同一故乡的人**；但如果他们旅行国外，在法国等**欧洲**地区偶遇，他们的同地域性就会扩大成**同胞**。根据合理类推，所有出了欧洲在美洲等世界各地相遇的欧洲人，都要称**同乡**。英格兰、荷兰、德国、瑞典等国之于欧洲，其地位正如街之于镇、镇之于郡，只是面积有大有小，性质是一样的。跨洲的人是不会使用街坊、同

[①] 基督教内部互称弟兄姊妹，因为他们认为彼此是灵胞弟兄，所以潘恩的意思是，摆脱和英国的亲戚关系，转向更高层面和更大范围的宗教方面的亲缘关系。另外，美国的清教和英国国教不同。最初就是有一帮清教徒不满英国国教的束缚，为了以自己的方式信仰上帝而乘坐五月花号抵达美洲，成为这里的第一批移民。
[②] 去同一个教堂的人们所占的区域。

镇人这两个小词的。再说，美洲只有不到1/3的居民是英国后代，甚至本省①也是如此。所以，我谴责只称英格兰为母国或故国的说法，那是完全错误、自私、脑子笨和短见识的。

但即使我们承认自己都是英裔，又有什么意义呢？没有任何意义。英国公然向我们宣战，所以就消除了美洲人这一称呼以外的其他一切名号。说什么我们有责任服从，真够滑稽的。英格兰现在这一脉王室的第一任王（征服者威廉）是法国人，英格兰的半数贵族都是法国后裔，所以，以此类推，英格兰是不是该由法国统治？

关于英国和殖民地若同心则威力无穷的问题，已经说得够多了，说什么可以睥睨世界。但那只是个推测。战争胜负由天不由人。那种话本身没有任何价值。而且这个大陆绝对不愿意倾全地之民，去亚洲、非洲或欧洲帮英军打仗。

---

① 宾夕法尼亚州。

而且，睥睨世界和我们有什么关系？我们的计划是贸易，如果妥善打理，通商定能为我们赢得整个欧洲的好感和友谊，因为整个欧洲最关心的是把美洲变成一个**自由港**。美洲的通商是它永恒的护身符，而它在金银方面没什么出产，可以保证不招致侵略。

我要挑战那些热烈倡议顺服的人，请你指出美洲臣服于大不列颠有什么好处？我重复这个挑战，没有一丁点儿好处。我们的粮食在欧洲任何市场都能卖出好价格，进口货物也都得花钱，去哪儿买都一样。

但臣服所带来的伤害和损失是举不胜举的，我们对全人类的责任以及对自己的责任告诉我们要拒绝这个联合，因为对大不列颠的任何屈从和依附，都会直接把美洲卷进欧洲的纷扰和战争中去，使我们与各国为敌。我们本来没有什么理由去怨愤那些国家，它们本来是会向我们寻求友谊的。整个欧洲都是我们的贸易市场，所以我们不应当和其中任何部分形成偏私的关系。美洲的真正利益所在，是和欧洲的任何纷争撇清关系，但只要依附英国，它就成了英国政治天平上的一个小砝码，所以永远不可能置身事外。

欧洲王国密布，所以不可能长期保持和平，每当英格兰和任何一国开战，美洲的贸易就毁了，因为**它和英格兰的关系**。下一场战争未必就像上次①一样，如有差池，现在鼓吹议和的人到时就会希望分离了，因为在战争中保持中立会比参战更能保卫美洲的安全。所有正确合理的事情都在呼求分离，战死者的鲜血和内心哭泣的声音在喊着：**该是分手的时候了**。甚至万能的上帝让美洲在空间上远离英格兰，也是上天安排的一个有力证据，说明英格兰有权统治美洲绝不是上帝的安排。同样，发现美洲的时间也能增加这个论点的力量，各国移民杂居的情况也增加了它的说服力。宗教改革和发现美洲是前后脚的事。仿佛荣耀的万能之神有意为几年后受迫害的人们开辟一个避难所似的。一旦发生宗教迫害，各国既不会付出友谊，也不会提供安全。

---

① 英国对法国等的"七年战争"，英国胜了。

大不列颠对美洲的统治，是一种早晚要结束的政府形式。只要认真思考后就能预见，这种所谓"现行体制"只是临时性的，想明白这件痛苦的事情，人们还能有什么真正的快乐吗？作为父母，知道**这个政府**不会持久，无法保证可以遗馈子孙，也绝对高兴不起来。说白了，既然我们亏欠子孙的，现在就该担当起来，否则我们就是自私、卑鄙地利用他们了。只有把孩子们考虑进来，站在数年之后来观察现在，我们才能发现自己正确的责任范围。站在那样的高度就能看到一片全新的景色，而当下的我们则被恐惧和偏见蒙住了眼睛。

虽然我不想一竿子打倒一片，得罪不必要的人，但我倾向于相信，议和论的支持者大致可分为以下几类：利益相关者，不能信赖；心智弱的人，**没有能力**看透；偏执的人，**不愿意**看透；一部分自卑的人，过分认为欧洲世界有多好。最后这类人，故意判断错误，对美洲带来的伤害比前三类更多。

许多人不在最近的悲伤事件①现场附近生活，这真是好运，因为恶没有临到他们的门口，使**他们**切身感受到美洲的全部财产被危险裹挟。但让想象力把我们暂时带去波士顿吧，灾难现场可以教会我们智慧，告诉我们要和一个不能信任的政府永远断绝关系。那个不幸城市的居民几个月前还过着恬淡的生活，不愁吃喝，但现在除了待在家里饿死或外出乞讨外，没有其他选择了。如果留在城里，就有被朋友们的火枪攻击的危险，如果离开，就要被军队洗劫。在现在的环境中，他们是一群没有救赎希望的囚犯，到处互相抢劫也只是为了缓解饥饿，将遭遇两种军队的怒火。

生性呆滞的人总爱小看英国的冒犯，仍很乐观，常喊：**"来，来，这些都不算啥，我们还可以是朋友嘛。"** 但议和派，请你考查一下人类的感情和感觉，把和解主张放在天理的天平上量

① 七年战争胜利后，为了转嫁军费负担，英国加紧对北美殖民地的控制和压榨，招致全民抵制英货。1770年3月5日，驻扎在波士顿的英军向抗议人群开枪，打死数人，史称"波士顿惨案"。

1773年12月16日波士顿发生政治示威，几十个美洲人潜入英国商船，把价值1.5万英镑的342箱茶叶（东印度公司积存的旧茶，当时东印度公司有在北美殖民地贩卖茶叶的独家权利，当地居民无权贩卖私茶）倒入大海，史称"波士顿倾茶事件"。英国议会为了镇压，采取了一系列更加严厉的措施，导致波士顿人大面积饿死。

一量，然后告诉我，你真的还能热爱、尊敬并忠心侍奉那个在自己家乡的土地上杀人放火的强国？如果你做不到，还主张议和，那就是自欺欺人，我们的子孙会因为你们这种人的磨叽遭受灭顶之灾。现在你都无法热爱和尊敬英国，那将来呢？关系一定是牵强和畸形的，只能走一步看一步权宜行事，顷刻间就会破裂，比现在更糟糕。但如果你说："那些暴行也不是不可以忍受啊。"那我就要问了："你的房子烧掉了吗？你的财产当着你的面付之一炬了吗？你的妻子儿女流落街头、没吃没喝吗？那些父母儿女惨遭毒手，自己断胳膊断腿只身死里逃命的可怜人是你吗？"如果不是你，你就没有资格替他们下判断。如果那是你，结果你还可以和凶手握手言欢，那我就问了："你配做丈夫、父亲、朋友、恋人吗？"不管你这辈子是干什么的，都有一颗懦夫的心，拥有足够的谄媚精神。

这不是夸张，也不是煽风点火，而是用符合天理的正常情感和感情来看问题，没有正常的情感和感情，我们就无法履行人生的职责，也无法享受其幸福。我并不是要展示恐怖以激起复仇情绪，而是要把人们从非人的濒死麻木中唤醒，使其坚定地追求某个确定的目标。如果美洲不先用**磨叽**和**懦弱**打败了自己，英国或欧洲怎么会有胆来犯？如果利用得当，这个冬天可以抵一个时代，如果荒废和失去了，整个美洲都将遭不幸。浪费这样一个宝贵的重要季节，不论他是谁、做什么的，只要住在这片大陆上，任何惩罚都不为过。

认为美洲可以继续受制于海外强国的想法，是违反理性的，是违反宇宙秩序的，从古至今从未有过先例。[①]在英国，甚至最有自信的人也不会这么想。穷尽人类智慧，除分手外别无他法可保证美洲哪怕一年的安全。**当下**，议和就是个荒诞的梦。这种纽带遭天厌弃，再怎么胡诌也无法为它的存在找到理由。弥尔顿智慧地说："当死仇的伤刺到深处，就不可能产生真正的议和。"

所有以和平求和平的方式均告无效。请愿被一遍遍蔑然回绝，只让我们肯定了一点，只有反复的请愿最能煽起国王

---

① 意思是，只有美洲人有这种想法。

的虚荣，鼓励他们的自负。欧洲的国王争相成为专制国王，主要就是人民频繁请愿，看看丹麦和瑞典吧。所以，只有迎头痛击才会有结果。那么，以上帝之名，让我们一刀两断，不要再让子孙后代惨遭屠戮了，因为如果我们允许那种事情发生，父母和子女的概念就是扭曲、毫无意义的了。

有人说他们不会再这么干了。那纯粹是胡扯和幻想。我们在抗议印花税法时曾抱有这样的幻想，但一两年的时间就惊醒了我们的迷梦。我们怎么可以认为只要打败它一次，一个暴徒国家就绝对不会再次发难了？

社会管理方面，英国没有公正治理美洲的能力。美洲的事务越来越重大、繁杂，不是一个离我们这么遥远、对我们这样无知的强权用某种程度的权宜之计所能管理的。他们既然不能征服我们，就没有能力管理我们。为了一个报告或申请，都必须奔波三四千英里，四五个月才能等来批复，批复后又需要五六个月请上头解释是什么意思……这种事几年之内就会被认为是荒唐和幼稚的。曾经它挺合适的，现在是让它停止合适的时候了。

几个无法保护自己的小岛，是王国可以自行治理的正常对象；但认为区区弹丸岛国可以永远统治一个大洲，就的确有些荒唐感了。大自然从未造出过一个比主星更大的卫星，英格兰和美洲的关系，违反自然的一般规律，所以两者显然不是一个星系的。英格兰是欧洲那个星系的，美洲是自成一体的。

我不是被骄傲、地方主义或憎恨之心攫住，所以支持分离和独立论的。我绝对打心眼儿里认为，这是符合美洲的根本利益的。任何不符合**根本利益**的都是临时的，不能提供持久的繁荣，只是退缩，只是把刀剑留给子孙，但同时只要我们多做一点、多迈出一步就可以使美洲大陆成为全世界的荣耀。

既然英国没有表露任何让步的意思，我们可以确信，即使议和，所得条款也是美洲所无法接受的，任何方式都弥补不了我们被迫付出的生命和财产的代价。

　　奋斗的目标，总该和成本有一定的比例才行。撤掉诺斯[①]甚至撤掉整个可鄙的内阁，也抵不过我们所付出的巨大牺牲。如果仅仅通过暂停贸易，就能抗议并废除我们反对的一切法案，所付出和所收获的就成比例了。但现在整个大陆都被迫拿起武器，人人都成了民兵，目标只是反对一个卑鄙的内阁，这就显得很不值得了。如果我们所奋斗的目标只是废除法案，那这代价也太大了。正常地算一下，付出邦克山[②]一样的代价，竟然不是为了土地而是为了在法律上占一点儿便宜，真是蠢到家了。我一直认为美洲大陆的独立是迟早会实现的事，根据大陆最近的迅速成长来看，它不远了。所以，既然已经撕破脸，就根本没必要再吵了，如果不是真的只想打打嘴仗，时间就已经为我们下了定论了。不然，那就像控告一个租期将满的佃户侵权而花光地产一样，成本和所得差得太多了。

---

① 腓特烈·诺斯是英王乔治三世的一任首相。
② 马萨诸塞州波士顿港北方的小山，独立战争时期的一个战场。

在痛苦的1775年4月19日^①之前，没有人比我更渴望议和了，但一听到那天发生的事，我立刻永远否定了黑心、乖戾的英格兰法老^②。我鄙视那个卑鄙小人，他僭称**人民之父**，却冷酷地听着他们互相残杀的消息，灵魂上沾满了鲜血却可以坦然入睡。

而如果认为问题就算解决了，就此打住，结果会怎么样？我回答：结果会是整个大陆的毁灭，我有下面几个理由。

第一，统治权仍然掌握在英王手里，他会否决这片大陆的全部立法^③。既然他已经展示自己是自由的死敌，对专制权力无限渴望，那么他必然会，或者说难道他不会对北美十三州说"除非我高兴，你们制定的法律一律作废"？是否有哪个美洲居民无知到不知道按照所谓**现行宪法**，除经国王批准，美洲大陆不得制定任何法律？是否有谁蠢到看不出（根据已

---

① 800名全副武装的英国轻步兵向莱克星顿进发，北美民兵奋勇抗击。
② 在基督教体系中，法老代表专制、凶残等，这里指英王。
③ 虽然各州都有议会，但法案只有经过英国的批准才能成为法律。所以，美州没有立法权。

经发生的一切)除了那些满足**他**的目的的法律之外,他不允许我们制定任何法律? 在英格兰给我们制定的那些法律在制约我们,所以就跟完全没有法律一样,我们处于奴役之中。在解决了问题(有人这样说)后,难道还能怀疑国王不会全权施威,把这片大陆降低到无以复加的低等地位吗? 不前进,我们就会后退,也就是永远在争论,可笑地请愿。**我们**的强大已经到了英王所不希望的程度,难道将来他不会努力削弱我们吗? 总之一句话,一个嫉妒我们的繁荣的政府是否适合来统治我们? 答"不"的人都是**美洲独立派**,因为独立只是意味着我们可以制定自己的法律,而不是任凭大陆的最大敌人英王来吩咐我们:**"除了我喜欢的不准有任何法律。"**

你会说:国王在英格兰也有否决权,未经他同意,那里也无法立法。按正确的常理来说,一个21岁的小青年居然(这种事常常发生)对几百万比他年长和聪明的人说"我禁止你们的这个或那个议案成为法律",这是十分荒唐的。但是在这里我就不这么驳斥了,虽然我会在别处继续揭露那个说法的荒唐,这里我只说:英格兰是国王的权力所在地,美洲不是，所以情况完全不同。国王在**这里**拥有否决权，比在英格兰危险和致命十倍，因为在**那里**，他很难否决一个努力使英国成为国防强国的议案，但在美洲，他绝对无法忍受通过这样的议案。

美洲在英国的政治体系中居于次要地位，它维持**这片土地**的利益，不会越过对**本土**利益的满足。所以，它自己的利益会让它压制或至少阻挠**我们的利益**的增长，只要我们的增长不引起它的增长那就不值得增长。在这样一个二手政府的统治下，从近期事件来看，我们很快就会处于一种很妙的境地了！人们并不会因为换个叫法就从敌人变成朋友。为了展示当下的议和论的危险性，我断言：**英王现在的策略就是，取消恶法以加强他对北美十三州的统治，目的在于将来利用阴谋诡计完成那些无法在短期内用武力和暴力完成的事。**毁灭与议和如影随形。

第二，能预料到的最好谈判结果，至多还是一种临时的权宜之计，或者一种监国治理方式。它持续不了多久，殖民地迟早都会成熟，而成熟之前的总体面貌和形势都将是不安定和没有希望的。有产的移民不会选择到这样一个国家来，政府形式朝不保夕，每天都濒临动乱和骚动。现有居民将抓住机会处置产业，迅速撤离这片大陆。

但最有力的论据是，除了独立（即联合整个大陆的政府形式），没有任何办法可以维持大陆的和平，使其免遭内战之扰。我担心，一旦和英国议和，不知哪个州就会发生暴乱，后果可能远比英国的恶意更加致命。

英国的暴行摧毁了成千上万的人（很可能会有另外成千上万的人遭遇同样的命运），那些人的情感和我们这些没有受难的人不一样。他们**现在**拥有的只剩下自由了，他们牺牲了曾经享有的一切来换取自由，既然再没有什么可以失去的了，也就鄙视屈服了。殖民地人民对英国政府的整体态度，类似一个即将成年的青年，根本就不会对它有任何顾虑。一个不能带来和平的政府根本就不是政府，因为我们拿钱什么都换不来。请问：万一议和后第二天美洲就发生暴乱，那么只在纸面上有权力的英国会做什么？我听到有人说（我相信其中很多人说这话是没过脑子的）自己害怕独立，担心独立会带来美洲内战。不过脑子就蹦出来的说法很少是真对的，这里就是这个情况，因为缝补起来的纽带比独立更让人担心十倍。如果我是一个受害者，我就会抗议：我被人从房子和家里赶出来，我的财产都毁了，家乡都没了，作为一个人，一个还懂得疼的人，我绝对不同意议和的主张，也绝对不认为自己有义务支持议和。

十三州表现出了高度一致的精神面貌，准备服从一个大陆政府，这足以使每个明白事理的人感到放心和高兴。没有人有任何理由担心一个根本不成立的借口，即：万一哪个州想凌驾于其他州之上呢？这可真够幼稚和荒唐的。

我们彼此没有差别，自然不会产生地位高低的问题，完全的平等绝不会诱发地位的争夺。欧洲各共和国都很和平（而且我们可以说一直如此）。荷兰和瑞士既无内战又无对外战争。而君主政府的确不会长期和平，皇冠本身就是刺激国

内恶棍的诱因，王权自带的那种极度的傲慢和嚣张，有时会导致和其他强国关系断裂。共和政府是建立在自然原则之上的，所以能克服那种错误。

关于独立，如果真有什么可担心的地方，那就是还没有定下什么规划，人们还看不到出路。所以，为了给这件事起个头，我提出以下建议，同时坦承，我并不认为它们有多厉害，我只是抛砖引玉。将人们凌乱的思想搜集起来，可以做材料，聪明能干的人可以打磨，将其变成有用的东西。

大陆会议可以一年一开，并只设一个议长。代表分布要比现在更均衡，代表只处理本州的事务，受大陆会议的权力的节制。

每州应合理分成6、8或10个区，每区各派若干代表参加会议。每州至少30人，总人数至少390人。每届会议应以以下方式选出并议定议长。代表们第一次集会时，所有13个州抽签产生一个州，然后经全体投票从该州代表中选出一人为议长。在第二次会议中，仅从12个州中抽出一个，上届已经产生议长的州不在抽签之列，依次类推，直至所有13个州都轮过一遍。为了保证所通过的法律都合理且令人满意，会议代表的3/5才能称为多数。在这样一个公平组建的政府中，任何要挑唆不和的人，就和路西法反叛时一样，注定会失败的。

但谁来怎样发起，是一个很困难的问题，所以由介于统治者和被统治者之间，即大陆会议和人民之间的某个中间团体来操办，貌似最合理可取。那就先组织一个**大陆协商会**，以以下方式进行，有以下目的。

先组建一个大陆会议的委员会，由26名委员组成，即每州2人。该2人来自州议会或州制宪会议，州议会或州制宪会议设5个代表，从该州全民中产生，代表全州并对全州负责，这些代表由全州各地尽量多的（人数自行斟酌）合格选民在各州首府市镇选出，或者，如果为了更方便，代表也可以在该州两三处人口最集中的城镇选出。这样召开的会议可以集中行政事务的两大原则，**信息**和**权力**。大陆会议、各州议会或制宪会议成员，对国家事务有经验，所以会成为能干、有用的议员。而整体来说，因为都经人民授权，所以拥有真正合法的权力。

议员集会共议国是时，可以草拟一个**大陆宪章**或联合殖民地宪章（回应所谓英国大宪章），确定大陆会议议员、州议会议员的人数和选举方式、开会的日期，划定各自的行政和司法界线（要一直牢记，我们的力量是大陆范围的，不是单独的州的）。要按照良心的指示，为所有人保证自由和财产安全，以及宪章应含的其他必要事务，最重要的是保证信仰自由。之后上述协商会应立即解散，并根据上述宪章选出人员，作为大陆的临时立法者和政府。愿上帝赐予他们平安幸福，阿门。

如果此后为了某种目的委任某些人的话，我要摘录先贤**德拉戈内蒂**①论政府的句子并奉上。"政治学，"他说，"在于

————————

① 意大利法学家，《论美德与奖赏》。

确定什么是幸福和自由的真正要义。如果能发现一种政府模式，可以使国家以最小的代价为个体获取最大的幸福，那么发现者是值得永世感恩的。"

但有人说：美洲的王在哪儿呢？我告诉你，朋友，他在天上统治，不像英国皇家畜生那样残害人类。但是，让我们在世俗荣耀中也不要显得敷衍了事吧，要专门安排出一天来庄严地宣布宪章，宣布宪章以神法也就是圣经为根据，为宪章加冕。这样世界就会知道，如果说我们赞同有王，那么在美洲**法律就是王**。在专制政府中，王就是法，而在自由国家中，法应该是王，别无其他。但为了预防将来发生滥用，就应当在典礼结束时打碎王冠，把权力分散到有权享用的人们手中。

拥有自己的政府是我们的天赋权利。如果一个人仔细思考人间事物的多变，他就会相信，冷静审慎地组织我们自己的政体，掌握在自己手里，比把这样一个利害攸关的大事交给时间和机会，要智慧和安全得多。如果现在不走这一步，也许将来会出现一个马萨涅洛^①，抓住民众的动荡情绪，纠集不满者和亡命之徒，把政府权力据为己有，像洪水一样把美洲的自由一下冲光。

万一议和成功，美洲政府再次落入英国之手，动荡的局势就会引诱某个不顾一切的冒险家尝试运气，那时英国能给我们什么帮助呢？它可能还没得到消息，不幸就已经作就，而我们就会像英国本地人饱尝征服者威廉的压迫一样饱尝不幸了。你们现在反对独立的人，不知道自己在干什么，你们是企图让政府空置，打开一扇通向永恒暴政的门。把煽动印第安人和黑人起来消灭我们的野蛮恶势力逐出美洲大陆，成千上万的人，千千万万的人都认为这是光荣的。英国的残酷产生了双重的罪，它残忍地对待我们，又骗了他们。

理智禁止我们信任某些人。我们的情感受到了伤害，不停地告诉我们要厌恶他们，和这些人谈友谊，不是疯就是

① 马萨涅洛本是那不勒斯的渔夫，他在公共市场上鼓励同胞反对西班牙统治者，倡议起义，于是当天就成了国王。

蠢。我们之间残留的一点亲缘关系每天都在损耗，难道有什么理由期望，在关系结束时感情反而会提高，或者当两者的争执比以前严重十倍、要吵的话题也多出十倍时，反倒会更和睦？

你们这些向我们乱喷和谐和议和的人，能让过去重来吗？你们能把曾经的纯洁还给娼妓吗？所以你们也不可能使英国和美洲和好。现在最后的一根弦也断了，英国人正用语言攻击我们。有些伤害是天理难容的，如果天理宽恕了它们，那就不是天理了。丈夫不会原谅强奸自己妻子的人，美洲不会宽恕英国的杀人犯。万能的上帝把追求善良和智慧的情感永远种在我们心里，这种情感守护我们心中上帝的形象，使我们不同于兽群。如果我们不解爱恨，社会契约就会解体，正义就会在地球上绝迹或者只是偶尔光临。假如承受的伤害不能使我们奋起追求正义，盗贼和杀人犯就会多多逍遥法外。

啊，热爱人类的人们啊，既敢于反抗暴政又敢直面暴君的人们啊，站出来吧！旧世界处处都是压迫。自由被四处驱赶，亚洲和非洲早就放逐了它，欧洲视其为异物，英国已经对它下了逐客令。啊，接待这个逃亡者，立刻为人类准备一个避难所吧。

第四章

论美洲目前的能力，
附带一些杂感

无论在英国还是美洲，我从未遇到过一个人不坦承两国迟早是要分离的。而我们在努力证明美洲大陆的独立条件已经成熟（或所谓充分）时，展示了极高的理性。

既然所有人都认为应当如此，只是在时间问题上有出入，那么，为了不犯错，我们可以考察一下大势，尽量努力锚定**正确的**时机。但其实无须多讲，问题立刻就有了答案，因为**时机已经找到了我们**。大势，也就是美洲当下的完美融合，就说明了事实。

我们最大的力量不在于人多，而在于团结，虽然我们现在的人数足以对抗全世界的武力。美洲现在拥有世界各国中最大的正规武装部队，我们已经获得了这种力量。任何单独一州都无法自卫，只有整体联合起来才能做到。就这些州联合，不能多也不能少，否则结果都是致命的。我们的陆军已经够用。至于海军，只要大陆仍然受制于人，我们就不能蠢到不明白，英国不会允许我们训练一个美洲水兵的。所以，一百年后的海军也不会比现在进步多少。实际上，一百年后再建海军会比现在更难，因为这片土地上的木材①每天都在减少，最后剩下的那些都地处偏远难以采伐。

假使美洲的人口再密集些，当前形势下的苦难就难以忍受了，因为海港城镇越多，需要防守和放弃的就越多。我们现今的人口，和我们的需要完全相称，所有人都有用武之地。劳动人数的减少能产生一支军队，而军队的需要会创造一个新的行业。

我们没有债务，而为了争取独立所产生的债务将会成为我们崇高美德的纪念。如果能把一个形式稳定的政府、一个

————————————
① 当时的海船是用木材建造的，而不是钢铁。

与众不同的独立政体留给后代，用任何代价来换都不算大。
而如果只是为了废除几项恶法、与现在的内阁周旋，花几
百万就划不来了。那是在极端残忍地利用子孙后代，因为那
就是把最艰难的工作留给他们去做，把债务压在他们背上，
而他们得不到任何益处。有尊严的人是不屑于那种想法的，
那只能出目光短浅和无聊的政客。

　　大事一成，负一点儿债又有什么大不了的？任何国家都
应该有些债务。国债①是国家的团结力量，只要没有利息，
就绝不是件烦事。英国负债累累，超过1.4亿镑，利息高达
400万。负债的结果就是，它有一大支海军；美洲没有债务，
也没有海军；而我们只要花费英国国债的1/20就能创造出同
样大的一支海军。英国海军目前只值350万镑。

　　这本小册子的前两版出版时没有下列数字，现在列出，
证明对海军的上述估算是合理的。②

① 美国很富有，所以只向国内人民举债即可。
② 参见恩蒂克著《海军史》前言部分，第56页。

根据海军大臣波切特先生的计算，建造各级战船，包括桅、桁、帆、索的装备费，根据级别各配备8个月的军需，所需花费为：

战船上的火炮数	花费（英镑）
100	35,553
90	29,886
80	23,638
70	17,795
60	14,197
50	10,606
40	7,558
30	5,846
20	3,710

这样，我们很容易计算出整个英国海军的总价值或总造价，因为它在1757年鼎盛时期的火炮和战船情况为：

战船（艘）	级别	单价（英镑）	造价小计（英镑）
6	100门炮	35,553	213,318
12	90门炮	29,886	358,632
12	80门炮	23,638	283,656
43	70门炮	17,795	764,755

续表

战船（艘）	级别	单价（英镑）	造价小计（英镑）
35	60门炮	14,197	496,895
40	50门炮	10,606	424,240
45	40门炮	7,558	340,110
58	20门炮	3,710	215,180
85	护卫舰、爆破艇、消防艇的组合	2,000	170,000
枪炮维护			233,214
总计			3,500,000

　　世界上没有任何国家像美洲一样如此得享地利，依靠自己的力量就能建造一支舰队。它天然出产柏油、木材、钢铁和绳索，我们不用进口什么。荷兰人向西班牙人和葡萄牙人出租军舰赚了大钱，但原料却不得不进口。我们天然出产造舰队用的原料，所以应当把它看作一项商业。这是我们最能挣到的钱。舰队一旦建成，其价值远超成本。这是国家政策的一个好处，既有商业价值又有国防意义。让我们来建造吧，如果我们自己用不上也可以卖，这样就可以用真金白银来代替现行纸币了。

关于战船的人员配置问题，人们普遍犯了大错，其实用不着1/4的专业水手。**声威震八方的**私掠船"死神船长号"，在上次战争中经历了最激烈的战斗，船上水兵不到20人，虽然编制高达200人。几个能干、善于沟通的老兵就能教会许多积极的旱鸭子，迅速学会船上的一般工作。现在我们的木材无法运出，渔场不能开，水手和船匠失业，所以，这是我们开创海上事业千载难逢的好机会。40年前的新英格兰造过装有七八十门火炮的战船，为什么现在不能再造？造船是美洲最大的骄傲，总有一天会超过整个世界。东方大国多为内陆国，所以在造船方面无法和美洲媲美；非洲仍处于野蛮状态；而欧洲的任何国家都没有这样长的海岸线，国内也没有这么多的原料供给。大自然的赐予往往是吝啬的，它赐予此就会收走彼，唯独给了美洲两样。俄罗斯帝国幅员广阔，但几乎与海隔绝，它无垠的森林，它的柏油、钢铁和绳索只不过是商品罢了。

从安全方面说，难道我们不应该拥有舰队吗？我们现在已经不是60年前那个弱小的民族了，那时我们可以把财产放

在大街上甚至旷野中都很放心，不关门窗睡得也很香。现在
不一样了，我们有钱了，保护财产的方式也应当提高。12个
月前，一个普通的海盗就可以上溯特拉华河，向费城人任意
勒索一笔巨款，其他地区也可能发生这种事。而且，任何亡
命之徒只要用一艘14或16门炮的双桅船就能够洗劫整个大陆，
抢走五十万镑钱财。这些情况值得我们关注，指向了海防的
必要性。

　　有些人会说，和英国议和后，它就会来保护我们了。难
道我们竟蠢到指望英国会为了保护我们而在我们的港口里常
驻一支海军？常识告诉我们，一直企图镇压我们的那个大国，
是最不配来保卫我们的。它可能会打着友谊的旗号来攻打我
们，而我们经过长期的英勇抵抗，最后会被骗进另一个囚笼。
如果不允许英国军舰开进我们的港口，请问它又怎么保护我
们呢？远在三四千英里之外的海军几乎没有任何用处，而在
紧急事件中就完全没有用处。所以，如果我们将来仍然需要
受到保护，为什么不自己保护自己呢？

英国军舰的清单很长，个个很唬人，但随时可以投入使用的不足1/10；大量军舰其实早就不存在了，但只要那船还剩下一块木板，它就不会从册子里除名。可以使用的军舰中，能立刻调来美洲港口的不足1/5。东印度群岛、西印度群岛、地中海、非洲等英国企图控制的地区，都急需它的海军。我们心里有先入为主的想法，不愿仔细考虑，所以对英国海军有一种错误的印象，说起来好像我们要同时应对它的全部海军似的，认为我们必须拥有一支同样庞大的海军。瞬间建立那么庞大的海军是不切实际的，这个说法曾被一群伪装起来的托利党人利用，企图打击我们兴建海军的第一步。那种想法错得不能更错了，因为美洲只要拥有英国海军1/20的战船就完全可以和英国匹敌了。我们既没有也不想拥有别国的领土，所以全部的海军都可以用在自己的海岸线上。从长远看，我们拥有以一敌二的优势，对方在发起进攻之前必须航行三四千英里而来，而且还得奔波三四千英里回去修理和补充给养。虽然英国靠舰队可以切断我们和欧洲之间的贸易，但是，我们在切断英国和西印度群岛之间的贸易方面，力量也不弱。西印度群岛就在美洲边，完全处于美洲的控制之下。

　　如果真的认为不必维持常备海军，倒也可以指望另一些方法，在和平时期保持海战能力。如果奖励商人建造并使用装有二三十或四五十门炮的船（补贴费用以减少的载货量为依据），那么只要有五六十艘，外加一些一直值勤的警备舰，我们就可以维持充足的海军力量了。英国一处于和平之中就会有人大声抱怨，说舰队只是躺在船坞里慢慢锈蚀，而我们这么做则可以免除这种困扰。商业和国防两手抓，是对的政策，因为当力量和财富握手，我们就不必害怕外来的敌人了。

　　我们富产几乎所有国防用品。纤维植物茂盛得不得了，所以我们不缺绳索。我们的钢铁质量世界领先。我们的轻武器不比任何别国差。我们可以随意建造大炮。我们每天都在生产硝石和火药。我们的知识每个小时都在增加。坚定的意志是我们天生的性格，而勇气也从未舍弃我们。所以，我们还缺什么呢？为什么仍然犹犹豫豫？除了毁灭，我们想不出英国还能给我们带来什么。如果继续承认它可以统治美洲，这片大陆就没法再住了。猜忌会一直不断，暴乱会一直发生，到时谁来平息它们呢？谁会愿意冒着生命危险镇压自己的同胞使其在外国人面前屈服？宾夕法尼亚和康涅狄格之间关于未定疆界的争执，说明英国政府是没有意义的，并且充分证明了只有大陆政府能够管理大陆事务。

当下是最佳时机，还有另外一个原因。我们人口越少，无人居住的土地就越多，这些土地不会被国王浪费掉，赐给他那些毫无价值的侍从，所以可以用来偿付当下的债务，同时可以长期资助政府。天底下没有任何另外一个国家有这样的地利。

殖民区的所谓婴儿状态，是一个有利于而绝对不是不利于独立的因素。我们人够多了，如果再多一些，在团结上可能就会差一些。值得指出的是，一个国家的人口越多，军队就越小。从军人数量上来说，古代远比现代多，原因很明显。人一多就需要贸易，人们忙于此而无暇他顾。贸易会减弱精神——爱国精神和军防精神。而历史多次告诉我们，一个国家最勇敢的成就往往是在它的幼年时期取得的。随着贸易的增长，英国丧失了它的精神。伦敦市虽然人口众多，却像懦夫一样耐心忍受持续的侮辱。能够失去的越多，人便越不愿冒险。富人一般都是恐惧的奴隶，臣服于朝廷的权力，像狗一样颤抖着斗心眼儿。

青年时期是播种好习惯的季节，个人如此，国家亦如此。50年后再想建立统一的美洲政府，即使可能也是困难的。随着贸易和人口的增长，各种利益分歧会加剧，会产生矛盾。一个州可能会反对另一个州。能干的人蔑视互相帮衬，而傲慢愚蠢的人有点儿小成就就会自鸣得意，有识之士将悲痛地后悔：为什么先前没有形成联盟？所以，**现在**正是建立它的**正确时机**。幼年时建立的亲密关系和在患难中建立的友谊是最长久不变的。如果现在联合，就能有上述两个优点，我们还年轻并同遭不幸，而我们的团结已经抵抗住了重重灾难，打下了子孙后代足以为荣和纪念的基础。

而且，现在是个特殊的时期，一个国家只能有一次，即自己组织一个政府的时期。很多国家错过了机会，所以被迫接受征服者的法律，而不是为自身制定法律。它们先得接受一个国王，然后再组织政府，所以会首先制定统治的条款或宪章，然后委派人执行。这样就延续了另一个国家的弊端。所以我们要学聪明些，抓住现在的机会，**给政府一个正确的开端**。

　　征服者威廉占领英国后，用剑指着人民接受他的法律。如果我们不支持美洲政府占有合法的权威地位，就会面临一种危险，这个位置将会被某个幸运的恶棍占领，他会以威廉那种方式来对待我们。到那时我们的自由何在？财产还由自己掌控吗？至于宗教，我认为保护所有虔诚的公开信仰者是所有政府不可推卸的责任，我不知道政府在这方面还该干别的什么事。丢掉灵魂的不开放性和教义的自私性①（各种小家子气的人很不愿摆脱）吧，我们就能摆脱这方面的各种恐惧了。不信任是低等灵魂的伴侣，是所有美好社会生活的祸根。就我自己来说，我完全真心地相信，我们中间有各种各样的宗教信仰，那是上帝的意志。这给基督的仁爱提供了一个更

---

① 大部分宗教都排他。

加广阔的施展空间。假如我们的思考方式都一模一样，我们的信仰就缺少了检验的根据。根据自由意志的原则，我把人们之间各种各样的宗派，看作一个家庭中的孩子，其不同只是叫的名字不一样。

在第三章后半部分①，我对大陆宪章的属性抛出了几点想法（因为我只想抛砖引玉而不是制订计划），此处我冒昧再次提起这个话题。我认为宪章可以理解为一种神圣义务的盟约，所有人一同订立，维护不同团体的利益，无论是宗教方面，还是个人自由和财产方面。牢固的契约和合理的利益使友谊更加长久。

前面我也提过建立广泛、平等的代表制的必要性，没有比这更值得注意的政治问题了。只有几个选民是危险的，只有几个代表同样危险。而如果代表的人数不仅少，而且不平

---

① 原文为page forty，即第40页。

均，危险就会增大。我说一件事作为例证：当联合会①的请愿书送到宾夕法尼亚州议会时，只有28个议员出席，巴克斯县共8名代表一致投了反对票，切斯特县的7个人步了后尘，整个州就由区区两个县控制了。经常容易出现这种危险。那个议会在上次开会时，有人大放厥词，扬言要操控本州的代表，这同样应当使全体人民警觉，人们是怎样把权柄交到别人手上并失控的。几个人凑了一套约束代表们的指导意见，从理性和权责方面来说连小学生都会觉得可耻，但**一小部分人**，实际上是**极少数人**关起门来通过之后就提交给了议会，并**代表整个殖民区**通过了。而假如全殖民区的人民知道那个议会的那小部分人到底在必要的公共措施中夹杂了多少恶意，他们就会毫不犹豫地认为他们不配得到自己的委托。

燃眉之急常需便宜行事，但长此以往就会变成迫害。权宜行事和权利是两回事。当灾难突降美洲需要会商时，除了

---

② 指费城联合会。在动乱中，富兰克林于1747年发表了小册子《明摆着的事实》（*Plain Truth*），号召自主成立一个联合会，保卫费城。1776年成为革命团体，第二年更名为宾夕法尼亚义勇军（Pennsylvania Militia）。

从几个州议会中委派数人解决，没有更快捷或更适合应急的办法了。他们在工作中表现出的智慧曾使这片大陆免遭灭顶之灾。但我们不太可能永远越过**议会**，所有对良好秩序抱着美好愿望的人都必须承认，这样选人办事的方式是值得考虑的。我要向人类研究者们提出一个问题：同一群人既有代议权又有选举权，这种权力是不是太大了？我们为子孙后代做打算时应当牢记，美德并不遗传。

我们常从敌人那里得到警句箴言，常被他们犯的错吓得理智起来。康沃尔先生（财政部权臣）轻蔑地对待纽约议会的请愿书，因为他说那个议会只有26个人，他说这么一小撮人不能很适当地代表全体。我们感谢他这种言不由衷的实话。①

总之，不管部分人觉得这多奇怪，不管他们是不是愿意这么想，都没关系，我可以举出很多明摆着的、强有力的原

---

① 如果你愿意充分理解广泛和平等的代议制对于一个国家来说是何等重要，可以阅读伯格写的政治论文。——原注

因来证明，除了断然公开宣布独立，没有任何方法可以有效解决我们的问题。其中几点如下：

第一，按照国际惯例，当两国交战，可以由未卷入争端的第三国出面调解，提出和解的预备条款。但只要美洲仍自称英属，任何国家，无论它对我们怀有多少善意，都无权干预。所以，在目前的状况下，我们可以吵到永远。

第二，有人认为法国或西班牙会给我们提供某种帮助。如果我们只打算用这种外援来修复裂隙、加强英美关系，那种臆测就是不合情理的，因为其结果会损害那两个国家的利益。

第三，只要我们还自称英国臣民，在他国眼中我们就必须是"叛逆"。此先河一开，就给**他们自己的和平**带来些危险，因为他们的臣民也会揭竿起义。悖论不攻自破了。但是，一边抵抗一边臣服的高见，一般人应该是弄不懂的。

第四，我希望我们发表宣言，分送给各国宫廷，陈述我们承受的苦难以及我们努力补救却行之无效的和平手段，同时宣布，由于无法再在英廷的残酷统治下幸福安全地生活，我们被迫和它一刀两断，同时向所有宫廷保证我们对它们抱着和平的愿望，愿意和它们通商。对这片大陆来说，这样一个备忘录比运一船请愿书到英国去，能产生更好的效果。

我们现在名义上是英国臣民，他国不能将我们视为国家，所以我们无法有国事沟通。各国宫廷的惯例对我们不利，并将永远不利，直到我们独立，才能与他国并列。

建国的程序乍看起来貌似陌生、困难，但就像我们曾经走过的其他步骤一样，不久就会变得熟悉和可爱。美洲觉得自己就像一个这样的人，他一天天持续拖延一件不愉快的事，但他知道这件事迟早要办，他不愿意着手，却希望它早已办完，必须去办的想法又永远挥之不去。这种情况会在宣布独立后停止。

附 言

自从这本小册子初版，或者可以说就在出版当天，英王的演讲词出现在了这个城市。如果预言之神为这个作品接生，那么真是生在了一个再合适不过的关头，或说生在了适宜的时机。彼方的嗜血成性，证明我方必须把方针确定下来。人们从英王的演讲词中读出了报复，但它不但没有吓倒人们，反而为断然独立的原则铺平了道路。

在卑鄙邪恶的表演面前保持礼貌甚至保持缄默，无论动机如何，都算给了一点儿首肯，从而让自己人心寒。如果这句箴言是对的，那么我就要说：英王的演讲词是流氓的杰作，应当从那时起到现在都遭受议会和人民的普遍诅咒。如果一个国家的内部和平只能依靠他的**自制**（其实叫**国家性做作**更合适），那他就默默地鄙视某些事就行了，不必变着法子说讨厌我们，那个所谓的我们的和平与安全的守护神根本就没什么创新性。也许主要是因为这种小心翼翼的拐弯抹角，英王的演讲词才没有（今天之前）受到公众的谴责。那篇演讲词（如果可以叫演讲词的话）不过是对真理、人民幸福和人类生存的肆无忌惮的蓄意诽谤，是把活人当作祭品献给狂妄暴君的做作、傲慢的方式。但这种形式的人类大屠杀是国王们的一项特权和国王存在的必然结果，因为国王的存在**违反天理**，他们也就**不知天道**，虽然他们是**我们自己**创造出来的，他们却不知道**我们**，并成为他们的创造者的神。演讲词有一个优点，即它并非为欺骗作就，即使我们愿意上当也无法受骗。残忍和暴政就写在脸上，不容我们看不懂。每句话一读就让我们相信，赤身裸体在树林里打猎的印第安人，也不如英王那样野蛮和没有教养。

这篇阴险的狂吠——《英格兰人民致美洲居民书》，题目很能误导人，其代笔约翰·达尔林普尔爵士也许曾经想当然地认为，这里的人民会被他对一个国王的吹嘘吓到，所以描述了当前这个国王的本性（虽然他这招并不明智）。"但是，"作者说，"如果你想赞扬一个我们并无不满的内阁（指撤销印花税法案的罗金哈姆侯爵的内阁），但不颂扬那个君王，便有失公道，因为**只有经过他点头他们才被准许做任何事情。**"这是聪明的保王主义啊！这是赤裸裸的偶像崇拜。谁要能冷静地听完并相信了这堆东西，他就已经放弃了理性的权利，脱离了人类这个物种，应当被认为是这样一种东西：不仅放弃了人类应有的尊严，而且自贬于动物之属之下，像一条蛆虫一样在世上卑鄙地爬行。

但英格兰的国王说什么或做什么，现在都无所谓了，他恶毒地击穿了每项道德和人类契约，把天理和良知踩在脚下，并用满脑子的偏执、傲慢、残忍，为自己招致普遍的厌恶。**现在**美洲自寻出路符合它自身的利益。它已经拥有一个年轻的大家庭，照顾这个大家庭才是它的责任所在，而不是奉献出财产，去支持一个辱没了人类和基督徒之名的国家。你们的责任是守卫这个国家的精神，无论你是哪个宗派。如果你有信仰，便更应守卫公共自由。如果你们想保全自己的祖国不被欧洲玷污，你们一定要暗中渴望独立。不过，把精神层面的东西留在私下思考吧，我将仅对两个问题再多说几句。

第一，从英国独立出来，是美洲的利益所在。

第二，**议和还是独立**，到底哪种方案更容易、更可行（随便评论一下）？

在支持独立方面，如果我判断不错的话，我可以说出这片大陆上最能干、最有经验的那部分人的意见。他们对于这个问题的强烈情感还没有公开宣布。实际上这个主张是不证自明的，因为任何一个国家，如果处于附属他国的状态，商业受到限制，立法权受到压缩和钳制，它就永远不能拥有真正的地位。美洲还不知道什么是真正的繁荣，虽然它已有的进步在各国史上都无法比拟，但和它所能成就的比起来，它现在还是个孩子，只要它把立法权掌握在自己手里，而且应当掌握在自己手里。英国现在正傲慢地垂涎一个得到之后对它没什么好处的东西，而美洲却对一个问题犹豫不决，而一旦忽视这个问题必将导致它的毁灭。英国要得到好处，就得通过贸易而不是征服美洲，如果两国像法国和西班牙一样互相独立，贸易关系多半可以持续下去，因为就很多商品来说，彼此都是最好的互补市场。但这片土地的独立是目前最值得讨论的问题，或唯一值得讨论的问题，脱离英国或其他任何国家。就像其他一切被逼现身的真理一样，独立的需要将日益明显和强烈。

1. 因为迟早会走到那步。

2. 因为迁延的时间越长，完成就会越困难。

我参加公共或私人聚会时，常悄悄地注意那些不过脑子就高谈阔论的人们仿佛言之成理的谬论，并暗自窃笑。在我所听到的诸多谬论中，下面这条仿佛最常见，即，如果眼下这种破裂推迟四五十年再来，而不是发生在**现在**，美洲将更有把握摆脱附属状态。我对此的回答是，我们**当下**的军事能力来自在上次战争中获得的经验，再过四五十年这个能力就消失了。到那时这片大陆一个将军甚至一个军官都留不下，我们（或说我们的后代）将会像古印第安人一样变成军事白痴。如果仔细思考，单是这一点就能无可争辩地证明，现在比任何时候都更有利。所以论证就变成了这样：上次战争结束时，我们有了经验，但人数不够，而四五十年后，我们人数将够但缺乏经验；所以，适当的时机应当是介于两个极端之间的某个点，既保留了足够的经验，又有适当人数的增加。而这个时机就是现在。

请读者原谅我岔开话题，讨论下面这个问题，它不是我最初讨论的问题的顺延，说完后我们再回到正题。

万一我们和英国的关系修复，英国的王权仍然统治美洲（根据当下局势，英国正完全放弃这一点），我们就会剥夺自己偿还债务①（或将来也许要举的债）的能力。由于加拿大无

---

① 前面说，美洲没有债务，这里说有债务。解释是，本书初版为1776年1月，2月时已经是第2版了，所以本书的再版速度很快，而潘恩则把后加的新信息、新想法都罗列在了《附言》中。这也解释了这一章略显凌乱的原因。

理限制的增多，某些州的内陆土地的价值已经下降，仅为每百英亩5英镑。地价总计约合宾夕法尼亚币2500万以上；地产税^①以每英亩1便士计，年达200万英镑。

卖掉这些土地就可以还清债务，而不使任何人受累，保留的地产税逐年减轻，迟早将和政府的每年开支持平。债务还多久没有多大关系，只要卖地的钱用来还债就行，所有这些事，北美大陆暂时委托给了议会处理。

现在我开始谈第二个问题，即议和与独立哪种方案更容易、更切合实际（随便评论一下）？

凡是以天理为指导的人，是不容易被驳倒的，所以我这样**概括地回答：独立是唯一简单的路线，主动权掌握在我们手里；议和是一个非常困难和复杂的问题。要和一个背信弃义、反复无常的朝廷交涉，答案是确定无疑的。**

---

① 在美国，买了土地之后土地就私有了，但每年要交一定的税，就像买了房子后每年都要交房产税一样。

每个还能思考的人，都会认为北美大陆的现状真的岌岌可危，除了良心的保证和基础外，我们没有任何形式的权力，没有法律，没有政府。团结我们的只有空前的情感共鸣，但情感这种东西很容易改变，每个秘密的敌人都在力图瓦解它。我们现在的情况是，有立法机构但没有法律，有智慧但没有方案，有体制但名不正，而最令人吃惊的怪事是，实际上完全独立却拼命地想要做附属。这种情况是史无前例的，以前从未有过这种事，谁能预测将来会发生什么？在目前这种松散的体系下，任何人的财产都不安全。人民的精神非常涣散，也无人照管，他们看不到确定的未来，所以随着幻想或流言起伏不定。没有什么事算犯罪，没有什么事算叛国，所以每个人都认为自己可以随心所欲，为所欲为。假如托利党人知道那么干国家法律会剥夺其性命的话，就不敢气势汹汹地聚会了。在战斗中俘获的英国士兵和被逮捕的明火执仗的北美大陆居民之间要划清界线。前者是俘虏，后者是叛徒；一个要失去自由，一个要失去脑袋。

虽然我们有智慧，但在处理某些问题时却有一个明显的毛病，那就是优柔寡断，这助长了意见的分歧。大陆的皮带扣太松。如果不当机立断，什么都晚了，到时候我们将陷入一种既不能**议和**又无法**独立**的困境。国王和他的卑微的追随者们积极地玩着分裂大陆的老把戏，我们之中也不乏忙于散布似真而伪的谎言的出版商。几个月前在两家纽约报纸以及另两家报纸上发表的那封精心打造的伪善的信，证明有些人既无见识又不老实。

躲进洞里或角落里谈论议和是容易的。但那些人是否真的仔细考虑过这项任务有多难，如果大陆因而分裂会带来多大的危险？他们是否想过，各行各业的人们的情况和处境，包括他们自己的，都应当审慎考虑？他们是否设身处地地考虑过那些**已经**丧失了**一切**的受害者，和那些为了保卫自己的家乡而放弃一**切**的士兵？如果他们那愚蠢的稳健只能迎合他们自己的个人情况，而不管别人，结局将让他们相信，"他们只是在打自己的如意小算盘"。

　　有人说，让我们回到1763年的关系①中去吧。对此我这样回答：现在英国无权同意这种提议，它也不会自己提出来。但是，万一内阁同意了，我自然就要问：怎样才能使这样一个腐败、没有信用的朝廷说话算话？换一届内阁——不，即使内阁没换届，也会拒绝履行义务，谎称议案是用武力胁迫通过的，或当时通过那种议案本就不明智。那时我们怎么办？我们到哪儿去控诉国家？大炮为王冠做辩护律师，而判决诉讼的不是正义，而是战争之剑。要恢复1763年的关系，只把法律调回当时的状态是不够的，我们的财富也得调回去，当时的法律和当时的情况是一体的。现在，被烧毁和破坏的城镇都重新修建了，私人损失减少了，公共债务（为了保家卫国欠下的债务）还完了，如果不然，我们现在会比那个黄金时代坏上百万倍。这种提议要是一年前提出的话，也许还

① 1763年以前，美洲人以英国人自居，认为自己享有英国臣民的权利，并代表英国在美洲向法国开战。1963年英法"七年战争"结束，英国赢了，但战争损耗巨大。英国为了转嫁高额的战争代价，加强了对北美殖民地的权威和剥削，之后陆续制订了一系列经济法律，把美洲变成了廉价原料产地和剩余商品倾销地。美洲人突然意识到，自己为自己作为英国人感到自豪，但英国并不把自己当英国人看待，并用各种针对美洲的歧视法案把英国和美洲割裂开来。所以，以1763年为分割线，之前是民族自豪感，之后是激怒美洲人的一套恶法。所以，1763年的关系就是：没有任何恶法，美洲人为祖国英国奋勇作战并感到骄傲。

能使大陆人民全心全意接受，但现在为时已晚。"已经渡过卢比孔河了。"

　　另外，仅仅为了强制废除一条财政恶法而诉诸武力，就像用武力强迫服从恶法一样，似乎是为神法所不容的，而且违背人的感情。两种目标都不能说明手段正当，因为人的生命如此珍贵，不能浪费在这样的小事上。我们的人身都经受过暴力及其威胁，我们的财产都是被武装力量摧毁的。只有当火和剑侵略我们的国家时，才能使我们的良心觉得必须拿起武器。当我们必须拿起武器保护自己时，和英国的一切从属关系就已经停止了，应当认为美洲的独立可以追溯到**第一颗射向英国的子弹**[①]，那颗子弹就已经宣示了它的独立。历史是一条连贯的线，既不是任意画出的，也不会因个人的雄心而延长，它是由一串事件组成的，而作者并非北美十三州。

　　我用下述适时与充满善意的意见来结束我的论述。我们

① 莱克星顿的枪声。

应当思考，今后有三种方法可以完成独立，美洲的命运终将
归于**三者**之一。它们是：通过在大陆会议上合法呼吁，依靠
军事力量，或者依靠平民。但将来，**我们自己的**士兵也不一
定是合格公民，而人群也不一定总是有理智的人的集合；如
前所述，美德并不遗传，也不会永远不变。如果独立是由三
种方法中的第一个来实现的，我们就有满满的机会和来自各
方面的信心来建立世界上最高尚、最纯洁的政体，我们有能
力重建世界。从诺亚①时代到现在，还没有发生过今天这样
的情况。一个新世界的诞生近在咫尺，也许会有一族人，像
全欧洲那样多的一代新人，将在未来几个月的大事中获得他
们那份自由。这个念想真是棒极了。从这个角度来看，几个
懦夫或利益相关者跳上舞台，说几句毫无意义的风凉话，和
建造一个世界的事业比起来，该是多么微不足道、可笑和渺
小啊。

　　假使我们错过目前这个有利的美好时期，之后再用其他

---

① 请参照诺亚方舟的故事。

方法来完成独立，就必须对后果负责，或指责那些目光短浅的偏执之辈，他们总是不过脑子就贸然反对这个方法。支持独立的理由有很多，人们应当私下去想，而不是被公开地灌输。现在不是讨论要不要独立的时候，我们应当急切地想把它建立在稳固、安全和荣耀的基础上，并因为还没有着手而感到不安。每天都使我们更加相信它的必要性。甚至托利党（如果我们中还有这样的人的话）应该最热烈地提倡，因为最早的委员会①的建立使他们没激起民愤，所以他们应当认为，一个充满智慧、结构良好的政府体制，将是继续保护他们免遭民愤的唯一、确定的安全方法。**所以**，如果他们不够善良成为辉格党，也该通情达理，希望独立。

　　一句话，独立是把我们团结在一起的唯一**纽带**。我们的眼睛将能看清我们的目标，我们的耳朵不会再听信残暴诡诈的敌人的各种阴谋。而且，我们将能站在合理的立场上看待英国，因为我们有理由断言，英国王朝和北美大陆联邦讨论

---

① 指1772—1774年成立的通讯委员会，由北美十三州的地方革命政权组成。

和平条款，比与其口中的叛民讨论议和条件，面子上更过得去。正是我们的一拖再拖鼓励它希望征服，我们的退缩只是延长了战争。既然我们停止贸易以弥补我们的悲伤的措施没有产生好效果，现在不妨尝试另一种选择，我们自己来抚慰自己的创伤，然后主动重开贸易。英国的商人和理智人士仍然会支持我们，因为有贸易的和平，比没有贸易的战争要好得多。如果重开贸易的提议被拒绝，我们可以向其他国家提出。

我的论述就基于以上这些。因为没有人对本书前几版提出意见，反驳其中主张，那么这就可以作为反证，说明该主张无法反驳，或赞成的人太多而无法反对。**所以**，让我们不再互相猜忌或用怀疑的目光互相试探，让我们每个人都把真挚的友谊之手伸向邻居，一起画一条分割线，像特赦令一样，埋葬和忘记从前所有的纷争。让我们不再叫作辉格党和托利党，仅让一种称呼在我们中间回响：**一个好公民、坦率勇敢的朋友、人类权利的勇敢护卫者、自由独立的美洲联邦的勇敢护卫者。**

致贵格会①代表的公开信

致人民宗教团体贵格会的代表，并顺致那些关心最近名为"致**全体人民**，关于**国王**和**政府**以及现在在**美洲**四起的**暴乱**，重申**贵格会**信徒的**古老戒律**和**原则**"的出版物的人。

本信的作者是为数不多的那种人②，既不亵渎自己的宗派也不嘲笑其他宗派所以不侮辱信仰的人。从信仰角度讲，任何人只应为上帝负责，向上帝陈述，而不是人。③你们是宗教团体，不是政治团体，宣称信奉**沉默原则**，所以本不该参与政治，所以写这样的公开信，对世事指手画脚，是不应当的。而且你们没有合法权利，却僭称代表全体贵格会，所以本作者为了和你们并驾齐驱，被迫让自己代表所有支持"你们的戒律禁止的原则和作品"的人。他④选择这个特殊的立场，是为了让你们在他身上看到自己傲慢的性格，因为你们自己

① 基督教的一个宗派，是非常顺服的一派，主张无为。
② 意思是，对方并非如此。
③ 作为基督徒，人的美德、功劳、德行等，不必为人所知，只需要在末日审判时向上帝陈述即可。
④ 作者自己。

没在自己身上看到。其实，无论他还是你们，都没有权利或官方权利发表**政治声明**。

当人脱离正道，跌倒就是必然。声明的行文显然说明，你们作为宗教团体人士，显然不是干政治这一行的，因为，不管你们自己觉得它多么有条理，它实际上只是胡乱拼凑起正反两方面论据，并得出一个既不自然也不正确的结论。

前两页（总共不到四页）。措辞一如既往地谦恭，我们称赞它，因为和平不是贵格会特有的热爱和渴望，而是人类所有宗派的自然宗教理想。正是基于此，当我们奋力建立属于我们自己的独立政体时，抱持着最热切的希望、最伟大的目的和规划。**我们的规划是永久的和平。**我们厌倦了和英国做口舌之争，除了一刀两断看不到任何真正的出路。我们言行一致，所以为了迎来永远、不间断的和平，我们愿意承受当下的恶和重担。我们过去一直并将一直不懈地努力下去，扯断和切断使我们的土地浸满鲜血的纽带，只要名义上还有这种关系，就是致命的，它将来会给两个国家都带来不幸。

　　我们并非为复仇而战，也不是要征服谁，不是出于骄傲或狂热，我们并不是在用我们的舰队和军队侮辱世界，也不是要席卷全球去抢劫。我们在自家葡萄藤架下遭到了攻击，有人在我们自己的家里，在我们的土地上，对我们犯下了暴行。我们把那些敌人看作拦路抢劫和入室行凶的暴徒之属，而且自己没有文明的法律来捍卫自己，所以被迫诉诸武力的律法来惩戒他们，拿起剑对付当下局势中的锁链。也许当我们想到大陆各个部分的人民所遭受的屠戮和侮辱，更加心痛，比你们中的某些人有过之而无不及。但请注意，一定要保证你们的声明不是出于错误或建立在错误的基础上。请不要称我们为冷血的灵魂，宗教界，请做真正的**基督徒**，而不要**愚信**。

　　啊，你们选择性地应用了自己宣称的教义。如果**拿起武器**是罪恶的，那么**先拿起武器**的一方必然罪更大，主动攻击和被迫自卫之间有天壤之别。所以，如果你们真的在凭着良心布道，而不是想把自己的信仰变成政治木偶，请把同一信条投向我们的敌人，因为**他们同样荷枪实弹**。你们向我们证明，这封在伦敦圣詹姆斯区发表的公开信，对驻扎在波士顿的陆军司令们①、像强盗一样蹂躏我们的海岸线的海军司令们，以及以你们宣誓效忠的**那个人**的名义进行屠杀的暴徒们，是相当贴心的。如果你拥有像巴克利②一样真诚的灵魂，就会去让**你们的**国王忏悔了。你会告诉那个**皇家小人**他的罪孽，警告他会得到永久的毁灭。③最起码你不会偏心地只谩骂受到伤害和侮辱的一方，而是像忠诚的牧师一样，大声**谴责双方**。不要说你们曾经蒙难，也不要僭称我们也谴责动乱，那都是你们在自说自话。我们可以向全世界保证：我们不是因为你们是贵格会才针对你们，我们和你们辩论乃是因为你们假装自己是贵格会，其实你们**不是**。

---

① 英军在波士顿驻扎。

② 指罗伯特·巴克利。巴克利家族是苏格兰的一个大家族，贵格会世家，出过很多将领和银行家。老巴克利是最早的贵格会信徒，在复辟期间被投入监狱，被狱友（Laird of Swinton）感化皈依。他的大儿子罗伯特·巴克利继承了父亲的衣钵，并发扬光大。而二儿子大卫·巴克利最为人所知的业绩是创建了巴克莱（这时一般译作巴克莱）银行。

③ 巴克利对查理二世说："你已尝遍顺境逆境，你知道被祖国放逐意味着什么，你知道统治和被统治意味着什么，你知道坐在王座上的滋味。曾经被迫害过，你有理由懂得暴君如何同时被上帝和人民厌弃。在你的逆境中，我主耶稣将你时刻挂怀；如果经历了这些警告和明示，你仍不能全心侍奉他，一过去就将他忘怀，无休止地沉湎于贪婪和虚荣，那么伟大的旨意必然会判你有罪。为了抵御天磨，以及那些现在或将来会奉承你的人们的诱惑，以免你堕入邪恶，最佳和有效的方式就是，全心顺从你良心中的基督之光。它不会也永远不会奉承你，会让你在你的罪中受苦而不是安息。"

　　啊，从你们声明的某些部分和某些行为来看，你们的脑子似乎倾向于把罪恶的概念缩小为**拿起武器的行为**，而且只有人民拿起武器才是罪恶的。我们觉得你们好像把党派利益当作了良心，因为你们做事自相矛盾。我们根本无法相信你们作为羊皮的很多顾虑，因为我们明白那些顾虑是编造出来的，那些人一边大声指责这个世界的名利，一边步步紧跟，步伐如时间一般稳健，胃口像死神一样贪婪。

　　你们在第三页里引用了《旧约·箴言》中的话："人所行的若蒙耶和华喜悦，耶和华也使他的仇敌与他和好。"这句选得并不明智，自己给自己挖了坑，因为那不啻于证明，国王的行径（你本来渴望支持他的）**并没有**取悦我们的主，否则他的统治就会天下太平了。

　　现在我们来看你们的声明的后半部分，相比之下，前半部分仿佛只是个引言。"我们受感召陈明基督耶稣之光，我们摸着良心说，我们一向坚定地遵守教义：立王与废王、建立和停止政府都是上帝独有的权力，其原因只有他自己知道，

所以我们无权染指。**上帝喜悦地委派政府统治我们，我们不**
能忙于超出自己位置的事务，更不能谋划、试图破坏或推翻
任何一个。我们只能为国王祈祷，为我们国家的安全祈祷，
为所有人的幸福祈祷，这样我们就能过上和平宁静的生活，
纯洁地沐浴上帝的恩泽。"如果这**真的是**你们的教义，那为
什么自己不遵守？为什么你不把你们所谓"上帝的工."留给
上帝自己去做？同样的教义也叫你们不要插手，只需要耐心、
顺从地等待人民的所有行动尘埃落定，并接受结果作为上帝
对你们的旨意。所以，如果你们全心相信你们的**政治戒律**①
的内容，那有什么理由发表这样的东西？发表它恰巧证明，
你们要么不相信自己所宣称的话，要么没有足够的美德去实
践自己相信的东西。

　　贵格会信条有一种直接的倾向，使人成为沉默、无害的
臣民，无论什么样的政府在统治他们。如果立王与废王、建
立和停止政府都是上帝独有的权力，必不得为我们所夺，那

---

① "戒律"是宗教领域的术语，和政治不搭界。政治就是政治，宗教就是宗教，这
两者杂糅在一起，就像西装配棉鞋一样不搭调。

么，你们就会支持所有的事件，无论发生什么，国王遇到什么事都是上帝的工，和你们没有任何关系。**奥利弗·克伦威尔**会感谢你，因为**查理一世**并非为人所杀，而现在这个**在傲慢方面可与查理一世媲美的人**，是否也应当得到同样夭折的命运？那篇声明的作者和出版者，如果遵循其中的教义，必然应该为那样的结果喝彩。暴君不是被神力变没的，政府中的变化也只能借由人力产生，就是我们现在使用的这种方法。即使犹太人的分散各地，虽然被我们的救主预言，也是由武力实现的。所以，如果你们拒绝站在我们这边，那也不应该加入他们那边，只需默默地等待最终的结果，除非你们胆敢僭夺神权证明：万能的上帝创造新世界时把它放在最遥远的地方，和整个旧世界东西相隔，但他反对新世界脱离腐朽、堕落的英国朝廷。如果你们不能证明这一点，我说，你们一边鼓动和煽动人民"坚定地团结起来，憎恶那些文章和手段，因为它们显然证明了一种目的，企图斩断我们一直和大不列颠王国享有的幸福纽带，消除我们正当且必要的顺服，疏远所有合法归其统治的人们"，一边宣称自己遵循无为的原则，这怎么自圆其说？这真是重重地打了自己的脸啊！你们这些人，上一段还安静、顺服地把国王和政府的秩序、更迭、罢黜交在上帝的手里，现在就受同样教义的感召，把一部分事情揽在了自己手里。上面一字不差地从你们的声明中摘下来的结尾部分，到底从哪个方面遵循你们上面写下的教义了？前后分裂太明显，想假装看不见都难。它荒唐得让人笑不出来。这种东西只能出脑子发昏的人作就，垂死挣扎的政党的偏执与暴躁使其黑了心肠。你们怎么敢自称代表整个贵格会？你们只是其中一小派，一小搓唯恐天下不乱的人。

这样，对你们的声明的考查就结束了（我不是想让人们厌弃你们的作品，只是想让人们读读公正的评价），我只追加以下评论。"立王与废王"的意思非常明确，也就是使一个不是王的人成为王，或者罢黜一个国王。请问这句话和当下的局势有什么关系吗？我们既不想立王也不想推倒谁，我们跟立王、废王没有关系。所以，你们的声明从各个角度看都只是羞辱了自己的判断能力。除此之外还有三个原因也说明，还不如不发表呢。

首先，它似乎在贬低和指责所有其他宗派。当一个宗派成了一个政党，参与政治博弈，对教会的其他所有部分都有终极杀伤力。

其次，它说一个团体表示关切并授权他们发表，而实际上有大量贵格会弟兄反对发表政治声明。

最后，它有破坏大陆的和谐的倾向，而贵格会最近无私的慈善捐赠曾帮助加强各州的友谊。而维持大陆的和谐和友谊，是我们目前顶级重要的事情。

我不带愤怒和憎恨地说再见。我衷心希望，作为基督徒，作为人，你们可以永远充分自由地享受所有信仰权和公民权，并转身去帮助别人获得这些权利。但你们把自己变成了愚蠢的典范，混淆了宗教和政治，必将遭受所有美洲居民的否定和谴责。

CONTENTS

Introduction..108

Of the origin and design of government in general, with
concise remarks on the English constitution................110

Of monarchy and hereditary succession......................118

Thoughts on the present state of American affairs.........130

Of the present ability of America, with some miscellaneous
reflections 151

Appendix..165

Introduction

Perhaps the sentiments contained in the following pages, are not YET sufficiently fashionable to procure them general favour; a long habit of not thinking a thing WRONG, gives it a superficial appearance of being RIGHT, and raises at first a formidable outcry in defense of custom. But the tumult soon subsides. Time makes more converts than reason.

As a long and violent abuse of power, is generally the Means of calling the right of it in question (and in Matters too which might never have been thought of, had not the Sufferers been aggravated into the inquiry) and as the King of England has undertaken in his OWN RIGHT, to support the Parliament in what he calls THEIRS, and as the good people of this country are grievously oppressed by the combination, they have an undoubted privilege to inquire into the pretensions of both, and equally to reject the usurpation of either.

In the following sheets, the author has studiously avoided everything which is personal among ourselves. Compliments as well as censure to individuals make no part thereof. The wise, and the worthy, need not the triumph of a pamphlet; and those whose sentiments are injudicious, or unfriendly, will cease of themselves unless too much pains are bestowed upon their conversion.

The cause of America is in a great measure the cause of all mankind. Many circumstances has, and will arise, which are not local, but universal, and through which the principles of all Lovers of Mankind are affected, and in the Event of which, their Affections are interested. The laying a Country desolate with Fire and Sword, declaring War against the natural rights of all Mankind, and extirpating the Defenders thereof from the Face of the Earth, is the Concern of every Man to whom Nature has given the Power of feeling; of which Class, regardless of Party Censure, is the AUTHOR.

P.S. The Publication of this new Edition has been delayed, with a View of taking notice (had it been necessary) of any Attempt to refute the Doctrine of Independence. As no Answer has yet appeared, it is now presumed that none will, the Time needful for getting such a Performance ready for the Public being considerably past.

Who the Author of this Production is, is wholly unnecessary to the Public, as the Object for Attention is the DOCTRINE ITSELF, not the MAN. Yet it may not be unnecessary to say, That he is unconnected with any Party, and under no sort of Influence public or private, but the influence of reason and principle.

Philadelphia, February 14, 1776

Of the origin and design of government in general, with concise remarks on the English constitution

Some writers have so confounded society with government, as to leave little or no distinction between them; whereas they are not only different, but have different origins. Society is produced by our wants, and government by our wickedness; the former promotes our happiness POSITIVELY by uniting our affections, the latter NEGATIVELY by restraining our vices. The one encourages intercourse, the other creates distinctions. The first a patron, the last a punisher.

Society in every state is a blessing, but government even in its best state is but a necessary evil; in its worst state an intolerable one; for when we suffer, or are exposed to the same miseries BY A GOVERNMENT, which we might expect in a country WITHOUT GOVERNMENT, our calamity is heightened by reflecting that we furnish the means by which we suffer. Government, like dress, is the badge of lost innocence; the palaces of kings are built on the ruins of the bowers of paradise. For were the impulses of conscience clear, uniform, and irresistibly obeyed, man would need no other lawgiver; but that not being the case, he finds it necessary to surrender up a part of his property to furnish means for the protection of the rest; and this he is induced to do by the same prudence which in every other case advises him out of two evils to choose the least. WHEREFORE, security being the true design and end of government, it unanswerably follows, that whatever FORM thereof appears most likely to ensure it to us, with the least expense and greatest benefit, is preferable to all others.

In order to gain a clear and just idea of the design and end of government, let us suppose a small number of persons settled in some sequestered part of the earth, unconnected with the rest, they will then represent the first peopling of any country, or of the world. In this state of natural liberty, society will be their first thought. A thousand motives will excite them thereto, the strength of one man is so unequal to his wants, and his mind so unfitted for perpetual solitude, that he is soon obliged to seek assistance and relief of another, who in his turn requires the same. Four or five united would be able to raise a tolerable dwelling in the midst of a wilderness, but one man might labour out of the common period of life without accomplishing anything; when he had felled his timber he could not remove it, nor erect it after it was removed; hunger in the mean time would urge him from his work, and every different want call him a different way. Disease, nay even misfortune would be death, for though neither might be mortal, yet either would disable him from living, and reduce him to a state in which he might rather be said to perish than to die.

Thus necessity, like a gravitating power, would soon form our newly arrived emigrants into society, the reciprocal blessings of which, would supersede, and render the obligations of law and government unnecessary while they remained perfectly just to each other; but as nothing but heaven is impregnable to vice, it will unavoidably happen, that in proportion as they surmount the first difficulties of emigration, which bound them together in a common cause, they will begin to relax in their duty and attachment to each other; and this remissness will point out the necessity of establishing some form of government to supply the defect of moral virtue.

Some convenient tree will afford them a State-House, under the branches of which, the whole colony may assemble to deliberate on public matters. It is more than probable that their first laws will have the title only of REGULATIONS, and be enforced by no other penalty than public disesteem. In this first parliament every man, by natural right, will have a seat.

But as the colony increases, the public concerns will increase likewise, and the distance at which the members may be separated, will render it too inconvenient for all of them to meet on every occasion as at first, when their number was small, their habitations near, and the public concerns few and trifling. This will point out the convenience of their consenting to leave the legislative part to be managed by a select number chosen from the whole body, who are supposed to have the same concerns at stake which those who appointed them, and who will act in the same manner as the whole body would act, were they present. If the colony continues increasing, it will become necessary to augment the number of the representatives, and that the interest of every part of the colony may be attended to, it will be found best to divide the whole into convenient parts, each part sending its proper number;

and that the ELECTED might never form to themselves an interest separate from the ELECTORS, prudence will point out the propriety of having elections often; because as the ELECTED might by that means return and mix again with the general body of the ELECTORS in a few months, their fidelity to the public will be secured by the prudent reflection of not making a rod for themselves. And as this frequent interchange will establish a common interest with every part of the community, they will mutually and naturally support each other, and on this (not on the unmeaning name of king) depends the STRENGTH OF GOVERNMENT, AND THE HAPPINESS OF THE GOVERNED.

Here then is the origin and rise of government; namely, a mode rendered necessary by the inability of moral virtue to govern the world; here too is the design and end of government, viz. freedom and security. And however our eyes may be dazzled with show, or our ears deceived by sound; however prejudice may warp our wills, or interest darken our understanding, the simple voice of nature and of reason will say, it is right.

I draw my idea of the form of government from a principle in nature, which no art can overturn, viz. that the more simple any thing is, the less liable it is to be disordered; and the easier repaired when disordered; and with this maxim in view, I offer a few remarks on the so much boasted constitution of England. That it was noble for the dark and slavish times in which it was erected, is granted. When the world was overrun with tyranny the least remove therefrom was a glorious rescue. But that it is imperfect, subject to convulsions, and incapable of producing what it seems to promise, is easily demonstrated.

Absolute governments (though the disgrace of human nature) have this advantage with them, that they are simple; if the people suffer, they know the head from which their suffering springs, know likewise the remedy, and are not bewildered by a variety of causes and cures. But the constitution of England is so exceedingly complex, that the nation may suffer for years together without being able to discover in which part the fault lies; some will say in one and some in another, and every political physician will advise a different medicine.

I know it is difficult to get over local or long standing prejudices, yet if we will suffer ourselves to examine the component parts of the English constitution, we shall find them to be the base remains of two ancient tyrannies, compounded with some new republican materials.

FIRST— The remains of monarchial tyranny in the person of the king.

SECONDLY— The remains of aristocratical tyranny in the persons of the peers.

THIRDLY— The new republican materials in the persons of the commons, on whose virtue depends the freedom of England.

The two first, by being hereditary, are independent of the people; wherefore in a CONSTITUTIONAL SENSE they contribute nothing towards the freedom of the state.

To say that the constitution of England is a UNION of three powers reciprocally CHECKING each other, is farcical, either the words have no meaning, or they are flat contradictions.

To say that the commons is a check upon the king, presupposes two things:

FIRST— That the king is not to be trusted without being looked after, or in other words, that a thirst for absolute power is the natural disease of monarchy.

SECONDLY— That the commons, by being appointed for that purpose, are either wiser or more worthy of confidence than the crown.

But as the same constitution which gives the commons a power to check the king by withholding the supplies, gives afterwards the king a power to check the commons, by empowering him to reject their other bills; it again supposes that the king is wiser than those whom it has already supposed to be wiser than him. A mere absurdity!

There is something exceedingly ridiculous in the composition of monarchy; it first excludes a man from the means of information, yet empowers him to act in cases where the highest judgment is required. The state of a king shuts him from the world, yet the business of a king requires him to know it thoroughly; wherefore the different parts, by unnaturally opposing and destroying each other, prove the whole character to be absurd and useless.

Some writers have explained the English constitution thus: The king, say they, is one, the people another; the peers are a house in behalf of the king, the commons in behalf of the people; but this has all the distinctions of a house divided against itself; and though the expressions be pleasantly arranged, yet when examined, they appear idle and ambiguous; and it will always happen, that the nicest construction that words are capable of, when applied to the description of something which either cannot exist, or is too incomprehensible to be within the compass of description, will be words of sound only, and though they may amuse the ear, they cannot inform the mind, for this explanation includes a previous question, viz. HOW CAME THE KING BY A POWER WHICH THE PEOPLE ARE AFRAID TO TRUST, AND ALWAYS OBLIGED TO CHECK? Such a power could not be the gift of a wise people, neither can any power, WHICH NEEDS CHECKING, be from God; yet the provision, which the constitution makes, supposes such a power to exist.

But the provision is unequal to the task; the means either cannot or will not accomplish the end, and the whole affair is a felo de se; for as the greater weight will always carry up the less, and as all the wheels of a machine are put in motion by one, it only remains to know which power in the constitution has the most weight, for that will govern; and though the others, or a part of them, may clog, or, as the phrase is, check the rapidity of its motion, yet so long as they cannot stop it, their endeavours will be ineffectual; the first moving power will at last have its way, and what it wants in speed, is supplied by time.

That the crown is this overbearing part in the English constitution, needs not be mentioned, and that it derives its whole consequence merely from being the giver of places and pensions, is self-evident, wherefore, though we have been wise enough to shut and lock a door against absolute monarchy, we at the same time have been foolish enough to put the crown in possession of the key.

The prejudice of Englishmen in favour of their own government by king, lords, and commons, arises as much or more from national pride than reason. Individuals are undoubtedly safer in England than in some other countries, but the WILL of the king is as much the LAW of the land in Britain as in France, with this difference, that instead of proceeding directly from his mouth, it is handed to the people under the more formidable shape of an act of parliament. For the fate of Charles the First has only made kings more subtle— not more just.

Wherefore, laying aside all national pride and prejudice in favour of modes and forms, the plain truth is, that IT IS WHOLLY OWING TO THE CONSTITUTION OF THE PEOPLE, AND NOT TO THE CONSTITUTION OF THE GOVERNMENT, that the crown is not as oppressive in England as in Turkey.

An inquiry into the CONSTITUTIONAL ERRORS in the English form of government is at this time highly necessary; for as we are never in a proper condition of doing justice to others, while we continue under the influence of some leading partiality, so neither are we capable of doing it to ourselves while we remain fettered by any obstinate prejudice. And as a man, who is attached to a prostitute, is unfitted to choose or judge a wife, so any prepossession in favour of a rotten constitution of government will disable us from discerning a good one.

Of monarchy and hereditary succession

Mankind being originally equals in the order of creation, the equality could only be destroyed by some subsequent circumstance; the distinctions of rich, and poor, may in a great measure be accounted for, and that without having recourse to the harsh, ill-sounding names of oppression and avarice. Oppression is often the CONSEQUENCE, but seldom or never the MEANS of riches; and though avarice will preserve a man from being necessitous poor, it generally makes him too timorous to be wealthy.

But there is another and greater distinction, for which no truly natural or religious reason can be assigned, and that is, the distinction of men into KINGS and SUBJECTS. Male and female are the distinctions of nature, good and bad the distinctions of heaven; but how a race of men came into the world so exalted above the rest, and distinguished like some new species, is worth inquiring into, and whether they are the means of happiness or of misery to mankind.

In the early ages of the world, according to the scripture chronology, there were no kings; the consequence of which was, there were no wars;

it is the pride of kings which throw mankind into confusion. Holland without a king has enjoyed more peace for this last century than any of the monarchial governments in Europe. Antiquity favours the same remark; for the quiet and rural lives of the first patriarchs has a happy something in them, which vanishes away when we come to the history of Jewish royalty.

Government by kings was first introduced into the world by the Heathens, from whom the children of Israel copied the custom. It was the most prosperous invention the Devil ever set on foot for the promotion of idolatry. The Heathens paid divine honours to their deceased kings, and the Christian world has improved on the plan, by doing the same to their living ones. How impious is the title of sacred majesty applied to a worm, who in the midst of his splendor is crumbling into dust!

As the exalting one man so greatly above the rest cannot be justified on the equal rights of nature, so neither can it be defended on the authority of scripture; for the will of the Almighty, as declared by Gideon and the prophet Samuel, expressly disapproves of government by kings. All anti-monarchical parts of scripture have been very smoothly glossed over in monarchical governments, but they undoubtedly merit the attention of countries which have their governments yet to form. RENDER UNTO CAESAR THE THINGS WHICH ARE CAESAR'S is the scripture doctrine of courts, yet it is no support of monarchical government, for the Jews at that time were without a king, and in a state of vassalage to the Romans.

Now three thousand years passed away from the Mosaic account of the creation, till the Jews under a national delusion requested a king. Till then their form of government (except in extraordinary cases, where the Almighty interposed) was a kind of republic administered by a judge and the elders of the tribes. Kings they had none, and it was held sinful to acknowledge any being under that title but the Lord of Hosts. And when a man seriously reflects on the idolatrous homage which is paid to the persons of kings, he need not wonder that the Almighty, ever jealous of his honour, should disapprove of a form of government which so impiously invades the prerogative of heaven.

Monarchy is ranked in scripture as one of the sins of the Jews, for which a curse in reserve is denounced against them. The history of that transaction is worth attending to.

The children of Israel being oppressed by the Midianites, Gideon marched against them with a small army, and victory, through the divine interposition, decided in his favour. The Jews, elate with success, and attributing it to the generalship of Gideon, proposed making him a king, saying, RULE THOU OVER US, THOU AND THY SON AND THY SON'S SON. Here was temptation in its fullest extent; not a kingdom only, but a hereditary one, but Gideon in the piety of his soul replied, I WILL NOT RULE OVER YOU, NEITHER SHALL MY SON RULE OVER YOU, THE LORD SHALL RULE OVER YOU. Words need not be more explicit; Gideon does not decline the honour, but denies their right to give it; neither does he compliment them with invented declarations of his thanks, but in the positive style of a prophet charges them with disaffection to their proper Sovereign, the King of heaven.

About one hundred and thirty years after this, they fell again into the same error. The hankering which the Jews had for the idolatrous customs of the Heathens, is something exceedingly unaccountable; but so it was, that laying hold of the misconduct of Samuel's two sons, who were entrusted with some secular concerns, they came in an abrupt and clamorous manner to Samuel, saying, BEHOLD THOU ART OLD, AND THY SONS WALK NOT IN THY WAYS, NOW MAKE US A KING TO JUDGE US, LIKE ALL OTHER NATIONS. And here we cannot but observe that their motives were bad, viz. that they might be LIKE unto other nations, i.e. the Heathens, whereas their true glory laid in being as much UNLIKE them as possible. BUT THE THING DISPLEASED SAMUEL WHEN THEY SAID, GIVE US A KING TO JUDGE US; AND SAMUEL PRAYED UNTO THE LORD, AND THE LORD SAID UNTO SAMUEL, HEARKEN UNTO THE VOICE OF THE PEOPLE IN ALL THAT THEY SAY UNTO THEE, FOR THEY HAVE NOT REJECTED THEE, BUT THEY HAVE REJECTED ME, THAT I SHOULD NOT REIGN OVER THEM. ACCORDING TO ALL THE WORKS WHICH THEY HAVE SINCE THE DAY THAT I BROUGHT THEM UP OUT OF EGYPT, EVEN UNTO THIS DAY; WHEREWITH THEY HAVE FORSAKEN ME AND SERVED OTHER GODS; SO DO THEY ALSO UNTO THEE. NOW THEREFORE HEARKEN UNTO THEIR VOICE, HOWBEIT, PROTEST SOLEMNLY UNTO THEM AND SHOW THEM THE MANNER OF THE KING THAT SHALL REIGN OVER THEM, I.E. not of any particular king, but the general manner of the kings of the earth, whom Israel was so eagerly copying after. And notwithstanding the great distance of time and difference of manners, the character is still in fashion. AND SAMUEL TOLD ALL THE WORDS OF THE LORD UNTO THE PEOPLE, THAT ASKED OF HIM A KING. AND HE SAID, THIS SHALL BE THE MANNER OF THE KING

THAT SHALL REIGN OVER YOU; HE WILL TAKE YOUR SONS AND APPOINT THEM FOR HIMSELF, FOR HIS CHARIOTS, AND TO BE HIS HORSEMAN, AND SOME SHALL RUN BEFORE HIS CHARIOTS (this description agrees with the present mode of impressing men) AND HE WILL APPOINT HIM CAPTAINS OVER THOUSANDS AND CAPTAINS OVER FIFTIES, AND WILL SET THEM TO EAR HIS GROUND AND REAP HIS HARVEST, AND TO MAKE HIS INSTRUMENTS OF WAR, AND INSTRUMENTS OF HIS CHARIOTS; AND HE WILL TAKE YOUR DAUGHTERS TO BE CONFECTIONARIES, AND TO BE COOKS AND TO BE BAKERS (this describes the expense and luxury as well as the oppression of kings) AND HE WILL TAKE YOUR FIELDS AND YOUR OLIVE YARDS, EVEN THE BEST OF THEM, AND GIVE THEM TO HIS SERVANTS; AND HE WILL TAKE THE TENTH OF YOUR SEED, AND OF YOUR VINEYARDS, AND GIVE THEM TO HIS OFFICERS AND TO HIS SERVANTS (by which we see that bribery, corruption, and favouritism are the standing vices of kings) AND HE WILL TAKE THE TENTH OF YOUR MEN SERVANTS, AND YOUR MAID SERVANTS, AND YOUR GOODLIEST YOUNG MEN AND YOUR ASSES, AND PUT THEM TO HIS WORK; AND HE WILL TAKE THE TENTH OF YOUR SHEEP, AND YOU SHALL BE HIS SERVANTS, AND YOU SHALL CRY OUT IN THAT DAY BECAUSE OF YOUR KING WHICH YOU SHALL HAVE CHOSEN, AND THE LORD WILL NOT HEAR YOU IN THAT DAY. This accounts for the continuation of monarchy; neither do the characters of the few good kings which have lived since, either sanctify the title, or blot out the sinfulness of the origin; the high encomium given of David takes no notice of him OFFICIALLY AS A KING, but only as a MAN after God's own heart. NEVERTHELESS THE PEOPLE REFUSED TO OBEY THE VOICE OF SAMUEL, AND THEY SAID, NAY, BUT WE WILL HAVE A KING OVER US, THAT WE MAY BE LIKE ALL THE NATIONS, AND THAT OUR KING MAY JUDGE US, AND GO OUT BEFORE US, AND FIGHT OUR BATTLES. Samuel continued to reason with them, but to no purpose; he set before them their ingratitude, but all would not avail; and seeing them fully bent on their folly, he cried out, I WILL CALL UNTO THE LORD, AND HE SHALL SEND THUNDER AND RAIN (which then was a punishment, being in the time of wheat harvest) THAT YOU MAY PERCEIVE AND SEE THAT YOUR WICKEDNESS IS GREAT WHICH YOU HAVE DONE IN THE SIGHT OF THE LORD, AND THE LORD SENT THUNDER AND RAIN THAT DAY, AND ALL THE PEOPLE GREATLY FEARED THE LORD AND SAMUEL. AND ALL THE PEOPLE SAID UNTO SAMUEL, PRAY FOR THY SERVANTS UNTO THE LORD THY GOD THAT WE DIE NOT, FOR WE HAVE ADDED UNTO OUR SINS THIS EVIL, TO ASK A KING. These portions of scripture are direct and positive. They admit of no equivocal construction. That the Almighty has here entered his protest against monarchical government, is true, or the scripture is false. And a man has good reason to believe that there is as much of kingcraft, as priestcraft, in withholding the scripture from the public in Popish countries. For monarchy in every instance is the Popery of government.

To the evil of monarchy we have added that of hereditary succession; and as the first is a degradation and lessening of ourselves, so the second, claimed as a matter of right, is an insult and an imposition on posterity. For all men being originally equals, no ONE by BIRTH could have a right to set up his own family in perpetual preference to all others forever, and though himself might deserve SOME decent degree of honours of his contemporaries, yet his descendants might be far too unworthy to inherit them. One of the strongest NATURAL proofs of the folly of hereditary right in kings, is, that nature disapproves it, otherwise she would not so frequently turn it into ridicule by giving mankind an ASS FOR A LION.

Secondly, as no man at first could possess any other public honours than were bestowed upon him, so the givers of those honours could have no power to give away the right of posterity. And though they might say, "We choose you for OUR head," they could not, without manifest injustice to their children, say, "that your children and your children's children shall reign over OURS forever." Because such an unwise, unjust, unnatural compact might (perhaps) in the next succession put them under the government of a rogue or a fool. Most wise men, in their private sentiments, have ever treated hereditary right with contempt; yet it is one of those evils, which when once established is not easily removed; many submit from fear, others from superstition, and the more powerful part shares with the king the plunder of the rest.

This is supposing the present race of kings in the world to have had an honourable origin; whereas it is more than probable, that could we take off the dark covering of antiquities, and trace them to their first rise, that we should find the first of them nothing better than the principal ruffian of some restless gang, whose savage manners or preeminence in subtlety obtained the title of chief among plunderers; and who by increasing in power, and extending his depredations, overawed the quiet and defenseless to purchase their safety by frequent contributions. Yet his electors could have no idea of giving hereditary right to his descendants, because such a perpetual exclusion of themselves was incompatible with the free and unrestrained principles they professed to live by. Wherefore, hereditary succession in the early ages of monarchy could not take place as a matter of claim, but as something casual or complemental; but as few or no records were extant in those days, and traditional history stuffed with fables, it was very easy, after the lapse of a few generations, to trump up some superstitious tale, conveniently timed, Mahomet like, to cram hereditary right down the throats of the vulgar. Perhaps the disorders which threatened, or seemed to threaten, on the decease of a leader and the choice of a new one (for elections among ruffians could not be very orderly) induced many at first to favour hereditary pretensions; by which means it happened, as it has happened since, that what at first was submitted to as a convenience, was afterwards claimed as a right.

England, since the conquest, has known some few good monarchs, but groaned beneath a much larger number of bad ones; yet no man in his senses can say that their claim under William the Conqueror is a very honourable one. A French bastard landing with an armed banditti, and establishing himself king of England against the consent of the natives, is in plain terms a very paltry rascally original. It certainly has no divinity in it. However, it is needless to spend much time in exposing the folly of hereditary right; if there are any so weak as to believe it, let them promiscuously worship the ass and lion, and welcome. I shall neither copy their humility, nor disturb their devotion.

Yet I should be glad to ask how they suppose kings came at first? The question admits but of three answers, viz. either by lot, by election, or by usurpation. If the first king was taken by lot, it establishes a precedent for the next, which excludes hereditary succession. Saul was by lot, yet the succession was not hereditary, neither does it appear from that transaction there was any intention it ever should be. If the first king of any country was by election, that likewise establishes a precedent for the next; for to say, that the RIGHT of all future generations is taken away, by the act of the first electors, in their choice not only of a king, but of a family of kings forever, has no parallel in or out of scripture but the doctrine of original sin, which supposes the free will of all men lost in Adam; and from such comparison, and it will admit of no other, hereditary succession can derive no glory. For as in Adam all sinned, and as in the first electors all men obeyed; as in the one all mankind were subjected to Satan, and in the other to Sovereignty; as our innocence was lost in the first, and our authority in the last; and as both disable us from reassuming some former state and privilege, it unanswerably follows that original sin and hereditary succession are parallels. Dishonourable rank! Inglorious connection! Yet the most subtle sophist cannot produce a juster simile.

As to usurpation, no man will be so hardy as to defend it; and that William the Conqueror was an usurper is a fact not to be contradicted. The plain truth is, that the antiquity of English monarchy will not bear looking into.

But it is not so much the absurdity as the evil of hereditary succession which concerns mankind. Did it ensure a race of good and wise men it would have the seal of divine authority, but as it opens a door to the FOOLISH, the WICKED, and the IMPROPER, it has in it the nature of oppression. Men who look upon themselves born to reign, and others to obey, soon grow insolent; selected from the rest of mankind their minds are early poisoned by importance; and the world they act in differs so materially from the world at large, that they have but little opportunity of knowing its true interests, and when they succeed to the government are frequently the most ignorant and unfit of any throughout the dominions.

Another evil which attends hereditary succession is, that the throne is subject to be possessed by a minor at any age; all which time the regency, acting under the cover of a king, have every opportunity and inducement to betray their trust. The same national misfortune happens, when a king, worn out with age and infirmity, enters the last stage of human weakness. In both these cases the public becomes a prey to every miscreant, who can tamper successfully with the follies either of age or infancy.

The most plausible plea, which has ever been offered in favour of hereditary succession, is, that it preserves a nation from civil wars; and were this true, it would be weighty; whereas, it is the most barefaced falsity ever imposed upon mankind. The whole history of England disowns the fact. Thirty kings and two minors have reigned in that distracted kingdom since the conquest, in which time there have been (including the Revolution) no less than eight civil wars and nineteen rebellions. Wherefore instead of making for peace, it makes against it, and destroys the very foundation it seems to stand on.

The contest for monarchy and succession, between the houses of York and Lancaster, laid England in a scene of blood for many years. Twelve pitched battles, besides skirmishes and sieges, were fought between Henry and Edward. Twice was Henry prisoner to Edward, who in his

128

turn was prisoner to Henry. And so uncertain is the fate of war and the temper of a nation, when nothing but personal matters are the ground of a quarrel, that Henry was taken in triumph from a prison to a palace, and Edward obliged to fly from a palace to a foreign land; yet, as sudden transitions of temper are seldom lasting, Henry in his turn was driven from the throne, and Edward recalled to succeed him. The parliament always following the strongest side.

This contest began in the reign of Henry the Sixth, and was not entirely extinguished till Henry the Seventh, in whom the families were united. Including a period of 67 years, viz. from 1422 to 1489.

In short, monarchy and succession have laid (not this or that kingdom only) but the world in blood and ashes. It's a form of government which the word of God bears testimony against, and blood will attend it.

If we inquire into the business of a king, we shall find that in some countries they have none; and after sauntering away their lives without pleasure to themselves or advantage to the nation, withdraw from the scene, and leave their successors to tread the same idle ground. In absolute monarchies the whole weight of business, civil and military, lies on the king; the children of Israel in their request for a king, urged this plea "that he may judge us, and go out before us and fight our battles." But in countries where he is neither a judge nor a general, as in England, a man would be puzzled to know what IS his business.

The nearer any government approaches to a republic the less business there is for a king. It is somewhat difficult to find a proper name for the government of England. Sir William Meredith calls it a republic; but in its present state it is unworthy of the name, because the corrupt influence of the crown, by having all the places in its disposal, has so effectually swallowed up the power, and eaten out the virtue of the house of commons (the republican part in the constitution) that the government of England is nearly as monarchical as that of France or Spain. Men fall out with names without understanding them. For it is the republican and not the monarchical part of the constitution of England which Englishmen glory in, viz. the liberty of choosing an house of commons from out of their own body— and it is easy to see that when republican virtue fails, slavery ensues. Why is the constitution of England sickly, but because monarchy has poisoned the republic, the crown has engrossed the commons?

In England a king has little more to do than to make war and give away places; which in plain terms, is to impoverish the nation and set it together by the ears. A pretty business indeed for a man to be allowed eight hundred thousand sterling a year for, and worshipped into the bargain! Of more worth is one honest man to society and in the sight of God, than all the crowned ruffians that ever lived.

Thoughts on the present state of American affairs

In the following pages I offer nothing more than simple facts, plain arguments, and common sense; and have no other Preliminaries to settle with the reader, than that he will divest himself of prejudice and prepossession, and suffer his reason and his feelings to determine for themselves; that he will put ON, or rather that he will not put OFF the true character of a man, and generously enlarge his views beyond the present day.

Volumes have been written on the subject of the struggle between England and America. Men of all ranks have embarked in the controversy, from different motives, and with various designs; but all have been ineffectual, and the period of debate is closed. Arms, as the last resource, decide this contest; the appeal was the choice of the king, and the continent has accepted the challenge.

It has been reported of the late Mr. Pelham (who though an able minister was not without his faults) that on his being attacked in the house of commons, on the score, that his measures were only of a temporary kind, replied "THEY WILL LAST MY TIME." Should a thought so fatal and unmanly possess the colonies in the present contest, the name of ancestors will be remembered by future generations with detestation.

The sun never shined on a cause of greater worth. It's not the affair of a city, a county, a province, or a kingdom, but of a continent— of at least one eighth part of the habitable globe. It's not the concern of a day, a year, or an age; posterity are virtually involved in the contest, and will be more or less affected, even to the end of time, by the proceedings now. Now is the seed-time of continental union, faith and honour. The least fracture now will be like a name engraved with the point of a pin on the tender rind of a young oak; the wound will enlarge with the tree, and posterity read it in full grown characters.

By referring the matter from argument to arms, a new era for politics is struck; a new method of thinking has arisen. All plans, proposals, etc. prior to the nineteenth of April, i. e. to the commencement of hostilities, are like the almanacs of the last year; which, though proper then are superseded and useless now. Whatever was advanced by the advocates on either side of the question then, terminated in one and the same point. viz. a union with Great Britain: the only difference between the parties was the method of effecting it; the one proposing force, the other friendship; but it has so far happened that the first has failed, and the second has withdrawn her influence.

As much has been said of the advantages of reconciliation which, like an agreeable dream, has passed away and left us as we were, it is but right, that we should examine the contrary side of the argument, and inquire into some of the many material injuries which these colonies sustain, and always will sustain, by being connected with, and dependent on Great Britain: To examine that connection and dependence, on the principles of nature and common sense, to see what we have to trust to, if separated, and what we are to expect, if dependant.

I have heard it asserted by some, that as America has flourished under her former connection with Great Britain that the same connection is necessary towards her future happiness, and will always have the same effect. Nothing can be more fallacious than this kind of argument. We may as well assert that because a child has thrived upon milk that it is never to have meat, or that the first twenty years of our lives is to become a precedent for the next twenty. But even this is admitting more than is true, for I answer roundly, that America would have flourished as much, and probably much more, had no European power had anything to do with her. The commerce, by which she has enriched herself, are the necessaries of life, and will always have a market while eating is the custom of Europe.

But she has protected us, say some. That she has engrossed us is true, and defended the continent at our expense as well as her own is admitted, and she would have defended Turkey from the same motive, viz. the sake of trade and dominion.

Alas, we have been long led away by ancient prejudices, and made large sacrifices to superstition. We have boasted the protection of Great Britain, without considering, that her motive was INTEREST not ATTACHMENT; that she did not protect us from OUR ENEMIES on OUR ACCOUNT, but from HER ENEMIES on HER OWN ACCOUNT, from those who had no quarrel with us on any OTHER ACCOUNT, and who will always be our enemies on the SAME ACCOUNT. Let Britain wave her pretensions to the continent, or the continent throw off the dependence, and we should be at peace with France and Spain were they at war with Britain. The miseries of Hanover last war ought to warn us against connections.

It has lately been asserted in parliament, that the colonies have no relation to each other but through the parent country, i. e. that Pennsylvania and the Jerseys, and so on for the rest, are sister colonies by the way of England; this is certainly a very round-about way of proving relationship, but it is the nearest and only true way of proving enemyship, if I may so call it. France and Spain never were, nor perhaps ever will be our enemies as AMERICANS, but as our being the subjects of GREAT BRITAIN.

But Britain is the parent country, say some. Then the more shame upon her conduct. Even brutes do not devour their young, nor savages make war upon their families; wherefore the assertion, if true, turns to her reproach; but it happens not to be true, or only partly so and the phrase PARENT or MOTHER COUNTRY has been Jesuitically adopted by the king and his parasites, with a low papistical design of gaining an unfair bias on the credulous weakness of our minds. Europe, and not England, is the parent country of America. This new world has been the asylum for the persecuted lovers of civil and religious liberty from EVERY PART of Europe. Hither have they fled, not from the tender embraces of the mother, but from the cruelty of the monster; and it is so far true of England, that the same tyranny which drove the first emigrants from home, pursues their descendants still.

In this extensive quarter of the globe, we forget the narrow limits of three hundred and sixty miles (the extent of England) and carry our friendship on a larger scale; we claim brotherhood with every European

Christian, and triumph in the generosity of the sentiment.

It is pleasant to observe by what regular gradations we surmount the force of local prejudice, as we enlarge our acquaintance with the world. A man born in any town in England divided into parishes, will naturally associate most with his fellow-parishioners (because their interests in many cases will be common) and distinguish him by the name of NEIGHBOUR; if he meet him but a few miles from home, he drops the narrow idea of a street, and salutes him by the name of TOWNSMAN; if he travel out of the county, and meet him in any other, he forgets the minor divisions of street and town, and calls him COUNTRYMAN, i. e. COUNTRYMAN; but if in their foreign excursions they should associate in France or any other part of EUROPE, their local remembrance would be enlarged into that of ENGLISHMEN. And by a just parity of reasoning, all Europeans meeting in America, or any other quarter of the globe, are COUNTRYMEN; for England, Holland, Germany, or Sweden, when compared with the whole, stand in the same places on the larger scale, which the divisions of street, town, and county do on the smaller ones; distinctions too limited for continental minds. Not one third of the inhabitants, even of this province, are of English descent. Wherefore I reprobate the phrase of parent or mother country applied to England only, as being false, selfish, narrow and ungenerous.

But admitting, that we were all of English descent, what does it amount to? Nothing. Britain, being now an open enemy, extinguishes every other name and title. And to say that reconciliation is our duty, is truly farcical. The first king of England, of the present line (William the Conqueror) was a Frenchman, and half the Peers of England are descendants from the same country; therefore, by the same method of reasoning, England ought to be governed by France.

Much has been said of the united strength of Britain and the colonies, that in conjunction they might bid defiance to the world. But this is mere presumption; the fate of war is uncertain, neither do the expressions mean anything; for this continent would never suffer itself to be drained of inhabitants, to support the British arms in either Asia, Africa, or Europe.

Besides what have we to do with setting the world at defiance? Our plan is commerce, and that, well attended to, will secure us the peace and friendship of all Europe; because, it is the interest of all Europe to have America a FREE PORT. Her trade will always be a protection, and her barrenness of gold and silver secure her from invaders.

I challenge the warmest advocate for reconciliation, to show, a single advantage that this continent can reap, by being connected with Great Britain. I repeat the challenge, not a single advantage is derived. Our corn will fetch its price in any market in Europe, and our imported goods must be paid for, buy them where we will.

But the injuries and disadvantages we sustain by that connection, are without number; and our duty to mankind at large, as well as to ourselves, instruct us to renounce the alliance: Because, any submission to, or dependence on Great Britain, tends directly to involve this continent in European wars and quarrels; and sets us at variance with nations, who would otherwise seek our friendship, and against whom, we have neither anger nor complaint. As Europe is our market for trade, we ought to form no partial connection with any part of it. It is the true interest of America to steer clear of European contentions, which she never can do, while by her dependence on Britain, she is made the make-weight in the scale of British politics.

Europe is too thickly planted with kingdoms to be long at peace, and whenever a war breaks out between England and any foreign power, the trade of America goes to ruin, BECAUSE OF HER CONNECTION WITH ENGLAND. The next war may not turn out like the last, and should it not, the advocates for reconciliation now, will be wishing for separation then, because, neutrality in that case, would be a safer convoy than a man of war. Everything that is right or natural pleads for separation. The blood of the slain, the weeping voice of nature cries, It's TIME TO PART. Even the distance at which the Almighty has placed England and America, is a strong and natural proof, that the authority of the one, over the other, was never the design of Heaven. The time likewise at which the continent was discovered, adds weight to the argument, and the manner in which it was peopled increases the force of it. The reformation was preceded by the discovery of America, as if the Almighty graciously meant to open a sanctuary to the Persecuted in future years, when home should afford neither friendship nor safety.

The authority of Great Britain over this continent, is a form of government, which sooner or later must have an end. And a serious mind can draw no true pleasure by looking forward under the painful and positive conviction, that what he calls "the present constitution" is merely temporary. As parents, we can have no joy, knowing that THIS GOVERNMENT is not sufficiently lasting to ensure anything which we may bequeath to posterity. And by a plain method of argument, as we are running the next generation into debt, we ought to do the work of it, otherwise we use them meanly and pitifully. In order to discover the line of our duty rightly, we should take our children in our hand, and fix our station a few years farther into life; that eminence will present a prospect, which a few present fears and prejudices conceal from our sight.

Though I would carefully avoid giving unnecessary offense, yet I am inclined to believe, that all those who espouse the doctrine of reconciliation, may be included within the following descriptions. Interested men, who are not to be trusted; weak men, who CANNOT see; prejudiced men, who WILL NOT see; and a certain set of moderate men, who think better of the European world than it deserves; and this last class, by an ill-judged deliberation, will be the cause of more calamities to this continent, than all the other three.

It is the good fortune of many to live distant from the scene of sorrow; the evil is not sufficient brought to their doors to make THEM feel the precariousness with which all American property is possessed. But let our imaginations transport us for a few moments to Boston, that seat of wretchedness will teach us wisdom, and instruct us forever to renounce a power in whom we can have no trust. The inhabitants of that unfortunate city, who but a few months ago were in ease and affluence, have now, no other alternative than to stay and starve, or turn and beg. Endangered by the fire of their friends if they continue within the city, and plundered by the soldiery if they leave it. In their present condition they are prisoners without the hope of redemption, and in a general attack for their relief, they would be exposed to the fury of both armies.

Men of passive tempers look somewhat lightly over the offenses of Britain, and, still hoping for the best, are apt to call out, "COME,

COME, WE SHALL BE FRIENDS AGAIN, FOR ALL THIS." But examine the passions and feelings of mankind, Bring the doctrine of reconciliation to the touchstone of nature, and then tell me, whether you can hereafter love, honor, and faithfully serve the power that has carried fire and sword into your land? If you cannot do all these, then are you only deceiving yourselves, and by your delay bringing ruin upon posterity. Your future connection with Britain, whom you can neither love nor honor will be forced and unnatural, and being formed only on the plan of present convenience, will in a little time fall into a relapse more wretched than the first. But if you say, you can still pass the violations over, then I ask, Has your house been burnt? Has your property been destroyed before your face! Are your wife and children destitute of a bed to lie on, or bread to live on? Have you lost a parent or a child by their hands, and yourself the ruined and wretched survivor! If you have not, then are you not a judge of those who have. But if you have, and still can shake hands with the murderers, then are you unworthy of the name of husband, father, friend, or lover, and whatever may be your rank or title in life, you have the heart of a coward, and the spirit of a sycophant.

This is not inflaming or exaggerating matters, but trying them by those feelings and affections which nature justifies, and without which, we should be incapable of discharging the social duties of life, or enjoying the felicities of it. I mean not to exhibit horror for the purpose of provoking revenge, but to awaken us from fatal and unmanly slumbers, that we may pursue determinately some fixed object. It is not in the power of Britain or of Europe to conquer America, if she do not conquer herself by DELAY and TIMIDITY. The present winter is worth an age if rightly employed, but if lost or neglected, the whole continent will partake of the misfortune; and there is no punishment which that man will not deserve, be he who, or what, or where he will, that may be the means of sacrificing a season so precious and useful.

It is repugnant to reason, to the universal order of things, to all examples from former ages, to suppose, that this continent can longer remain subject to any external power. The most sanguine in Britain does not think so. The utmost stretch of human wisdom cannot, at this time, compass a plan short of separation, which can promise the continent even a year's security. Reconciliation is NOW a fallacious dream. Nature has deserted the connection, and Art cannot supply her place. For, as Milton wisely expresses, "Never can true reconcilement grow, where wounds of deadly hate have pierced so deep."

Every quiet method for peace has been ineffectual. Our prayers have been rejected with disdain; and only tended to convince us, that nothing flatters vanity, or confirms obstinacy in Kings more than repeated petitioning— and nothing has contributed more than that very measure to make the Kings of Europe absolute. Witness Denmark and Sweden. Wherefore, since nothing but blows will do, for God's sake, let us come to a final separation, and not leave the next generation to be cutting throats, under the violated unmeaning names of parent and child.

To say, they will never attempt it again is idle and visionary, we thought so at the repeal of the stamp-act, yet a year or two undeceived us; as well may we suppose that nations, which have been once defeated, will never renew the quarrel.

As to government matters, it is not in the power of Britain to do this continent justice: The business of it will soon be too weighty, and intricate, to be managed with any tolerable degree of convenience, by a power so distant from us, and so very ignorant of us; for if they cannot conquer us, they cannot govern us. To be always running three or four thousand miles with a tale or a petition, waiting four or five months for an answer, which when obtained requires five or six more to explain it in, will in a few years be looked upon as folly and childishness— There was a time when it was proper, and there is a proper time for it to cease.

Small islands not capable of protecting themselves, are the proper objects for kingdoms to take under their care; but there is something very absurd, in supposing a continent to be perpetually governed by an island. In no instance has nature made the satellite larger than its primary planet, and as England and America, with respect to each other, reverses the common order of nature, it is evident they belong to different systems; England to Europe, America to itself.

I am not induced by motives of pride, party, or resentment to espouse the doctrine of separation and independence; I am clearly, positively, and conscientiously persuaded that it is the true interest of this continent to be so; that everything short of THAT is mere patchwork, that it can afford no lasting felicity, — that it is leaving the sword to our children, and shrinking back at a time, when, a little more, a little farther, would have rendered this continent the glory of the earth.

As Britain has not manifested the least inclination towards a compromise, we may be assured that no terms can be obtained worthy the acceptance of the continent, or any ways equal to the expense of blood and treasure we have been already put to.

The object, contended for, ought always to bear some just proportion to the expense. The removal of North, or the whole detestable junto, is a matter unworthy the millions we have expended. A temporary stoppage of trade, was an inconvenience, which would have sufficiently balanced the repeal of all the acts complained of, had such repeals been obtained; but if the whole continent must take up arms, if every man must be a soldier, it is scarcely worth our while to fight against a contemptible ministry only. Dearly, dearly, do we pay for the repeal of the acts, if that is all we fight for; for in a just estimation, it is as great a folly to pay a Bunker-hill price for law, as for land. As I have always considered the independency of this continent, as an event, which sooner or later must arrive, so from the late rapid progress of the continent to maturity, the event could not be far off. Wherefore, on the breaking out of hostilities, it was not worthwhile to have disputed a matter, which time would have finally redressed, unless we meant to be in earnest; otherwise, it is like wasting an estate on a suit at law, to regulate the trespasses of a tenant, whose lease is just expiring. No man was a warmer wisher for reconciliation than myself, before the fatal nineteenth of April 1775, but the moment the event of that day was made known, I rejected the hardened, sullen tempered Pharaoh of England forever; and disdain the wretch, that with the pretended title of FATHER OF HIS PEOPLE can unfeelingly hear of their slaughter, and composedly sleep with their blood upon his soul.

But admitting that matters were now made up, what would be the event? I answer, the ruin of the continent. And that for several reasons.

FIRST. The powers of governing still remaining in the hands of the king, he will have a negative over the whole legislation of this continent. And as he has shown himself such an inveterate enemy to liberty, and discovered such a thirst for arbitrary power; is he, or is he not, a proper man to say to these colonies, "YOU SHALL MAKE NO LAWS BUT WHAT I PLEASE." And is there any inhabitant in America so ignorant as not to know, that according to what is called the PRESENT CONSTITUTION, that this continent can make no laws but what the king gives leave to; and is there any man so unwise, as not to see, that (considering what has happened) he will suffer no law to be made here, but such as suit HIS purpose. We may be as effectually enslaved by the want of laws in America, as by submitting to laws made for us in England. After matters are made up (as it is called) can there be any doubt, but the whole power of the crown will be exerted, to keep this continent as low and humble as possible? Instead of going forward we shall go backward, or be perpetually quarrelling or ridiculously petitioning. — WE are already greater than the king wishes us to be, and will he not hereafter endeavour to make us less? To bring the matter to one point. Is the power who is jealous of our prosperity, a proper power to govern us? Whoever says No to this question, is an INDEPENDANT, for independency means no more, than, whether we shall make our own laws, or whether the king, the greatest enemy this continent has, or can have, shall tell us "THERE SHALL BE NO LAWS BUT SUCH AS I LIKE."

But the king you will say has a negative in England; the people there can make no laws without his consent. In point of right and good order, there is something very ridiculous, that a youth of twenty-one (which has often happened) shall say to several millions of people, older and wiser than himself, I forbid this or that act of yours to be law. But in this place I decline this sort of reply, though I will never cease to expose the absurdity of it, and only answer, that England being the King's residence, and America not so, makes quite another case. The king's negative HERE is ten times more dangerous and fatal than it can be in England, for THERE he will scarcely refuse his consent to a bill for putting England into as strong a state of defense as possible, and in America he would never suffer such a bill to be passed.

America is only a secondary object in the system of British politics, England consults the good of THIS country, no farther than it answers her OWN purpose. Wherefore, her own interest leads her to suppress the growth of OURS in every case which does not promote her advantage, or in the least interferes with it. A pretty state we should soon be in under such a secondhand government, considering what has happened! Men do not change from enemies to friends by the alteration of a name. And in order to show that reconciliation now is a dangerous doctrine, I affirm, THAT IT WOULD BE POLICY IN THE KING AT THIS TIME, TO REPEAL THE ACTS FOR THE SAKE OF REINSTATING HIMSELF IN THE GOVERNMENT OF THE PROVINCES; in order, that HE MAY ACCOMPLISH BY CRAFT AND SUBTLETY, IN THE LONG RUN, WHAT HE CANNOT DO BY FORCE AND VIOLENCE IN THE SHORT ONE. Reconciliation and ruin are nearly related.

SECONDLY. That as even the best terms, which we can expect to obtain, can amount to no more than a temporary expedient, or a kind of government by guardianship, which can last no longer than till the colonies come of age, so the general face and state of things, in the interim, will be unsettled and unpromising. Emigrants of property will not choose to come to a country whose form of government hangs but by a thread, and who is every day tottering on the brink of commotion and disturbance; and numbers of the present inhabitants would lay hold of the interval, to dispense of their effects, and quit the continent.

But the most powerful of all arguments, is, that nothing but independence, i.e. a continental form of government, can keep the peace of the continent and preserve it inviolate from civil wars. I dread the event of a reconciliation with Britain now, as it is more than probable, that it will be followed by a revolt somewhere or other, the consequences of which may be far more fatal than all the malice of Britain.

Thousands are already ruined by British barbarity; (thousands more will probably suffer the same fate.) Those men have other feelings than us who have nothing suffered. All they NOW possess is liberty, what they before enjoyed is sacrificed to its service, and having nothing more to lose, they disdain submission. Besides, the general temper of the colonies, towards a British government, will be like that of a youth, who is nearly out of his time; they will care very little about her. And a government which cannot preserve the peace, is no government at all, and in that case we pay our money for nothing; and pray what is it that Britain can do, whose power will be wholly on paper, should a civil tumult break out the very day after reconciliation! I have heard some men say, many of whom I believe spoke without thinking, that they dreaded an independence, fearing that it would produce civil wars. It is but seldom that our first thoughts are truly correct, and that is the case here; for there are ten times more to dread from a patched up connection than from independence. I make the sufferers case my own, and I protest, that were I driven from house and home, my property destroyed, and my circumstances ruined, that as man, sensible of injuries, I could never relish the doctrine of reconciliation, or consider myself bound thereby.

The colonies have manifested such a spirit of good order and obedience to continental government, as is sufficient to make every reasonable person easy and happy on that head. No man can assign the least pretence for his fears, on any other grounds, than such as are truly childish and ridiculous, viz. that one colony will be striving for superiority over another.

Where there are no distinctions there can be no superiority, perfect equality affords no temptation. The republics of Europe are all (and we may say always) in peace. Holland and Switzerland are without wars, foreign or domestic. Monarchical governments, it is true, are never long at rest; the crown itself is a temptation to enterprising ruffians at HOME; and that degree of pride and insolence ever attendant on regal authority, swells into a rupture with foreign powers, in instances, where a republican government, by being formed on more natural principles, would negotiate the mistake.

If there is any true cause of fear respecting independence, it is because no plan is yet laid down. Men do not see their way out— Wherefore, as an opening into that business, I offer the following hints; at the same time modestly affirming, that I have no other opinion of them myself, than that they may be the means of giving rise to something better. Could the straggling thoughts of individuals be collected, they would frequently form materials for wise and able men to improve into useful matter.

LET the assemblies be annual, with a President only. The representation more equal. Their business wholly domestic, and subject to the authority of a Continental Congress.

Let each colony be divided into six, eight, or ten, convenient districts, each district to send a proper number of delegates to Congress, so that each colony send at least thirty. The whole number in Congress will be at least 390. Each Congress to sit and to choose a president by the following method. When the delegates are met, let a colony be taken from the whole thirteen colonies by lot, after which, let the whole Congress choose (by ballot) a president from out of the delegates of that province. In the next Congress, let a colony be taken by lot from twelve only, omitting that colony from which the president was taken in the former Congress, and so proceeding on till the whole thirteen shall have had their proper rotation. And in order that nothing may pass into a law but what is satisfactorily just not less than three fifths of the Congress to be called a majority— He that will promote discord, under a government so equally formed as this, would have joined Lucifer in his revolt.

But as there is a peculiar delicacy, from whom, or in what manner, this business must first arise, and as it seems most agreeable and consistent, that it should come from some intermediate body between the governed and the governors, that is, between the Congress and the people. Let a CONTINENTAL CONFERENCE be held, in the following manner, and for the following purpose.

A committee of twenty-six members of Congress, viz. two for each colony. Two Members from each House of Assembly, or Provincial Convention; and five representatives of the people at large, to be chosen in the capital city or town of each province, for and in behalf of the whole province, by as many qualified voters as shall think proper to attend from all parts of the province for that purpose; or, if more convenient, the representatives may be chosen in two or three of the most populous parts thereof. In this conference, thus assembled, will be united, the two grand principles of business KNOWLEDGE and POWER. The members of Congress, Assemblies, or Conventions, by having had experience in national concerns, will be able and useful counselors, and the whole, being empowered by the people, will have a truly legal authority.

The conferring members being met, let their business be to frame a CONTINENTAL CHARTER, or Charter of the United Colonies; (answering to what is called the Magna Carta of England) fixing the number and manner of choosing members of Congress, members of Assembly, with their date of sitting, and drawing the line of business and jurisdiction between them (Always remembering, that our strength is continental, not provincial). Securing freedom and property to all men, and above all things, the free exercise of religion, according to the dictates of conscience; with such other matter as is necessary for a charter to contain. Immediately after which, the said Conference to dissolve, and the bodies which shall be chosen comfortable to the said charter, to be the legislators and governors of this continent for the time being: Whose peace and happiness may God preserve, Amen.

Should any body of men be hereafter delegated for this or some similar purpose, I offer them the following extracts from that wise observer on governments DRAGONETTI. "The science," says he, "of the politician consists in fixing the true point of happiness and freedom. Those men would deserve the gratitude of ages, who should discover a mode of government that contained the greatest sum of individual happiness, with the least national expense."

But where, says some, is the King of America? I'll tell you. Friend, he reigns above, and does not make havoc of mankind like the Royal Brute of Britain. Yet that we may not appear to be defective even in earthly honors, let a day be solemnly set apart for proclaiming the charter; let it be brought forth placed on the divine law, the word of God; let a crown be placed thereon, by which the world may know, that so far as we approve of monarchy, that in America THE LAW IS KING. For as in absolute governments the King is law, so in free countries the law OUGHT to be King; and there ought to be no other. But lest any ill use should afterwards arise, let the crown at the conclusion of the ceremony, be demolished, and scattered among the people whose right it is.

A government of our own is our natural right. And when a man seriously reflects on the precariousness of human affairs, he will become convinced, that it is infinitely wiser and safer, to form a constitution of our own in a cool deliberate manner, while we have it in our power, than to trust such an interesting event to time and chance. If we omit it now, some Massanello may hereafter arise, who laying hold of popular disquietudes, may collect together the desperate and the discontented, and by assuming to themselves the powers of government, may sweep away the liberties of the continent like a deluge. Should the government of America return again into the hands of Britain, the tottering situation of things will be a temptation for some desperate adventurer to try his fortune; and in such a case, what relief can Britain give? Ere she could hear the news, the fatal business might be done; and ourselves suffering like the wretched Britons under the oppression of the Conqueror. You that oppose independence now, you know not what you do; you are opening a door to eternal tyranny, by keeping vacant the seat of government. There are thousands, and tens of thousands, who would think it glorious to expel from the continent that barbarous and hellish power, which has stirred up the Indians and Negroes to destroy us; the cruelty has a double guilt, it is dealing brutally by us, and treacherously by them.

To talk of friendship with those in whom our reason forbids us to have faith, and our affections wounded through a thousand pores instruct us to detest, is madness and folly. Every day wears out the little remains of kindred between us and them, and can there be any reason to hope, that as the relationship expires, the affection will increase, or that we shall agree better, when we have ten times more and greater concerns to quarrel over than ever?

You that tell us of harmony and reconciliation, can you restore to us the time that is past? Can you give to prostitution its former innocence? Neither can you reconcile Britain and America. The last cord now is broken, the people of England are presenting addresses against us. There are injuries which nature cannot forgive; she would cease to be nature if she did. As well can the lover forgive the ravisher of his mistress, as the continent forgive the murders of Britain. The Almighty has implanted in us these unextinguishable feelings for good and wise purposes. They are the guardians of his image in our hearts. They distinguish us from the herd of common animals. The social compact would dissolve, and justice be extirpated the earth, or have only a casual existence were we callous to the touches of affection. The robber, and the murderer, would often escape unpunished, did not the injuries which our tempers sustain, provoke us into justice.

O you that love mankind! You that dare oppose, not only the tyranny, but the tyrant, stand forth! Every spot of the old world is overrun with oppression. Freedom has been hunted round the globe. Asia, and Africa, have long expelled her— Europe regards her like a stranger, and England has given her warning to depart. O! receive the fugitive, and prepare in time an asylum for mankind.

Of the present ability of America, with some miscellaneous reflections

I have never met with a man, either in England or America, who has not confessed his opinion that a separation between the countries, would take place one time or other. And there is no instance, in which we have shown less judgement, than in endeavouring to describe, what we call the ripeness or fitness of the Continent for independence.

As all men allow the measure, and vary only in their opinion of the time, let us, in order to remove mistakes, take a general survey of things, and endeavour, if possible, to find out the VERY time. But we need not go far, the inquiry ceases at once, for, the TIME HAS FOUND US. The general concurrence, the glorious union of all things prove the fact.

It is not in numbers, but in unity, that our great strength lies; yet our present numbers are sufficient to repel the force of all the world. The Continent has, at this time, the largest body of armed and disciplined men of any power under Heaven; and is just arrived at that pitch of strength, in which no single colony is able to support itself, and the whole, when united, can accomplish the matter, and either more, or, less than this, might be fatal in its effects. Our land force is already sufficient, and as to naval affairs, we cannot be insensible, that Britain would never suffer an American man of war to be built, while the continent remained in her hands. Wherefore, we should be no forwarder an hundred years hence in that branch, than we are now; but the truth is, we should be less so, because the timber of the country is every day diminishing, and that, which will remain at last, will be far off and difficult to procure.

Were the continent crowded with inhabitants, her sufferings under the present circumstances would be intolerable. The more seaport towns we had, the more should we have both to defend and to lose. Our present numbers are so happily proportioned to our wants, that no man need be idle. The diminution of trade affords an army, and the necessities of an army create a new trade.

Debts we have none; and whatever we may contract on this account will serve as a glorious memento of our virtue. Can we but leave posterity with a settled form of government, an independent constitution of its own, the purchase at any price will be cheap. But to expend millions for the sake of getting a few vile acts repealed, and routing the present ministry only, is unworthy the charge, and is using posterity with the utmost cruelty; because it is leaving them the great work to do, and a debt upon their backs, from which they derive no advantage. Such a thought is unworthy of a man of honor, and is the true characteristic of a narrow heart and a peddling politician.

The debt we may contract does not deserve our regard, if the work be but accomplished. No nation ought to be without a debt. A national debt is a national bond; and when it bears no interest, is in no case a grievance. Britain is oppressed with a debt of upwards of one hundred and forty millions sterling, for which she pays upwards of four millions interest. And as a compensation for her debt, she has a large navy; America is without a debt, and without a navy; yet for the twentieth part of the English national debt, could have a navy as large again. The navy of England is not worth, at this time, more than three millions and an half sterling.

The first and second editions of this pamphlet were published without the following calculations, which are now given as a proof that the above estimation of the navy is just.

The charge of building a ship of each rate, and furnishing her with masts, yards, sails and rigging, together with a proportion of eight months boatswain's and carpenter's seastores, as calculated by Mr. Burchett, Secretary to the navy.

	Pounds sterling
For a ship of a 100 guns	35,553
90	29,886
80	23,638
70	17,795
60	14,197
50	10,606
40	7,558
30	5,846
20	3,710

And from hence it is easy to sum up the value, or cost rather, of the whole British navy, which in the year 1757, when it was at its greatest glory consisted of the following ships and guns:

Ships	Guns	Cost of one	Cost of all
6	100	35,553	213,318
12	90	29,886	358,632
12	80	23,638	283,656
43	70	17,785	764,755
35	60	14,197	496,895
40	50	10,606	424,240
45	40	7,558	340,110
58	20	3,710	215,180
85	Sloops, bombs and fireships, one with another	2,000	170,000
Cost 3,266,786			
Remains for guns			233,214
			3,500,000

No country on the globe is so happily situated, or so internally capable of raising a fleet as America. Tar, timber, iron, and cordage are her natural produce. We need go abroad for nothing. Whereas the Dutch, who make large profits by hiring out their ships of war to the Spaniards and Portuguese, are obliged to import most of their materials they use. We ought to view the building a fleet as an article of commerce, it being the natural manufactory of this country. It is the best money we can lay out. A navy when finished is worth more than it cost. And is that nice point in national policy, in which commerce and protection are united. Let us build; if we want them not, we can sell; and by that means replace our paper currency with ready gold and silver.

In point of manning a fleet, people in general run into great errors; it is not necessary that one fourth part should be sailors. The Terrible privateer, Captain Death, stood the hottest engagement of any ship last war, yet had not twenty sailors on board, though her complement of men was upwards of two hundred. A few able and social sailors will soon instruct a sufficient number of active landmen in the common work of a ship. Wherefore, we never can be more capable to begin on maritime matters than now, while our timber is standing, our fisheries blocked up, and our sailors and shipwrights out of employ. Men of war of seventy and eighty guns were built forty years ago in New England, and why not the same now? Ship-building is America's greatest pride, and in which she will in time excel the whole world. The great empires of the east are mostly inland, and consequently excluded from the possibility of rivaling her. Africa is in a state of barbarism; and no power in Europe has either such an extent of coast, or such an internal supply of materials. Where nature has given the one, she has withheld the other; to America only has she been liberal of both. The vast empire of Russia is almost shut out from the sea; wherefore, her boundless forests, her tar, iron, and cordage are only articles of commerce.

In point of safety, ought we to be without a fleet? We are not the little people now, which we were sixty years ago; at that time we might have trusted our property in the streets, or fields rather; and slept securely without locks or bolts to our doors or windows. The case now is altered, and our methods of defense ought to improve with our increase of property. A common pirate, twelve months ago, might have come up the Delaware, and laid the city of Philadelphia under instant contribution, for what sum he pleased; and the same might have happened to other places. Nay, any daring fellow, in a brig of fourteen or sixteen guns might have robbed the whole continent, and carried off half a million of money. These are circumstances which demand our attention, and point out the necessity of naval protection.

Some, perhaps, will say, that after we have made it up with Britain, she will protect us. Can we be so unwise as to mean, that she shall keep a navy in our harbours for that purpose? Common sense will tell us, that the power which has endeavoured to subdue us, is of all others the most improper to defend us. Conquest may be effected under the pretence of friendship; and ourselves after a long and brave resistance, be at last cheated into slavery. And if her ships are not to be admitted into our harbours, I would ask, how is she to protect us? A navy three or four thousand miles off can be of little use, and on sudden emergencies, none at all. Wherefore, if we must hereafter protect ourselves, why not do it for ourselves?

The English list of ships of war, is long and formidable, but not a tenth part of them are at any one time fit for service, numbers of them not in being; yet their names are pompously continued in the list, if only a plank be left of the ship. And not a fifth part of such as are fit for service, can be spared on any one station at one time. The East and West Indies, Mediterranean, Africa, and other parts over which Britain extends her claim, make large demands upon her navy. From a mixture of prejudice and inattention, we have contracted a false notion respecting the navy of England, and have talked as if we should have the whole of it to encounter at once, and for that reason, supposed, that we must have one as large; which not being instantly practicable, have been made use of by a set of disguised Tories to discourage our beginning thereon. Nothing can be farther from truth than this; for if America had only a twentieth part of the naval force of Britain, she would be by far an overmatch for her; because, as we neither have, nor claim any foreign dominion, our whole force would be employed on our own coast, where we should, in the long run, have two to one the advantage of those who had three or four thousand miles to sail over, before they could attack us, and the same distance to return in order to refit and recruit. And although Britain, by her fleet, has a check over our trade to Europe, we have as large a one over her trade to the West Indies, which, by laying in the neighbourhood of the continent, is entirely at its mercy.

Some method might be fallen on to keep up a naval force in time of peace, if we should not judge it necessary to support a constant navy. If premiums were to be given to merchants, to build and employ in their service ships mounted with twenty, thirty, forty or fifty guns, (the premiums to be in proportion to the loss of bulk to the merchants) fifty or sixty of those ships, with a few guardships on constant duty, would keep up a sufficient navy, and that without burdening ourselves with the evil so loudly complained of in England, of suffering their fleet, in time of peace to lie rotting in the docks. To unite the sinews of commerce and defense is sound policy; for when our strength and our riches play into each other's hand, we need fear no external enemy.

In almost every article of defense we abound. Hemp flourishes even to rankness, so that we need not want cordage. Our iron is superior to that of other countries. Our small arms equal to any in the world. Cannon we can cast at pleasure. Saltpetre and gunpowder we are

158

every day producing. Our knowledge is hourly improving. Resolution is our inherent character, and courage has never yet forsaken us. Wherefore, what is it that we want? Why is it that we hesitate? From Britain we can expect nothing but ruin. If she is once admitted to the government of America again, this Continent will not be worth living in. Jealousies will be always arising; insurrections will be constantly happening; and who will go forth to quell them? Who will venture his life to reduce his own countrymen to a foreign obedience? The difference between Pennsylvania and Connecticut, respecting some unlocated lands, shows the insignificance of a British government, and fully proves, that nothing but Continental authority can regulate Continental matters.

Another reason why the present time is preferable to all others, is, that the fewer our numbers are, the more land there is yet unoccupied, which instead of being lavished by the king on his worthless dependants, may be hereafter applied, not only to the discharge of the present debt, but to the constant support of government. No nation under heaven has such an advantage at this.

The infant state of the Colonies, as it is called, so far from being against, is an argument in favour of independence. We are sufficiently numerous, and were we more so, we might be less united. It is a matter worthy of observation, that the more a country is peopled, the smaller their armies are. In military numbers, the ancients far exceeded the moderns: and the reason is evident. For trade being the consequence of population, men become too much absorbed thereby to attend to anything else. Commerce diminishes the spirit, both of patriotism and military defense. And history sufficiently informs us, that the bravest achievements were always accomplished in the non-age of a nation. With the increase of commerce, England has lost its spirit. The city of London, notwithstanding its numbers, submits to continued insults with the patience of a coward. The more men have to lose, the less willing are they to venture. The rich are in general slaves to fear, and submit to courtly power with the trembling duplicity of a Spaniel.

Youth is the seed time of good habits, as well in nations as in individuals. It might be difficult, if not impossible, to form the Continent into one government half a century hence. The vast variety of interests, occasioned by an increase of trade and population, would create confusion. Colony would be against colony. Each being able might scorn each other's assistance: and while the proud and foolish gloried in their little distinctions, the wise would lament, that the union had not been formed before. Wherefore, the PRESENT TIME is the TRUE TIME for establishing it. The intimacy which is contracted in infancy, and the friendship which is formed in misfortune, are, of all others, the most lasting and unalterable. Our present union is marked with both these characters: we are young and we have been distressed; but our concord has withstood our troubles, and fixes a memorable area for posterity to glory in.

The present time, likewise, is that peculiar time, which never happens to a nation but once, viz. the time of forming itself into a government. Most nations have let slip the opportunity, and by that means have been compelled to receive laws from their conquerors, instead of making laws for themselves. First, they had a king, and then a form of government; whereas, the articles or charter of government, should be formed first, and men delegated to execute them afterward but from the errors of other

nations, let us learn wisdom, and lay hold of the present opportunity—
TO BEGIN GOVERNMENT AT THE RIGHT END.

When William the Conqueror subdued England, he gave them law at the point of the sword; and until we consent, that the seat of government, in America, be legally and authoritatively occupied, we shall be in danger of having it filled by some fortunate ruffian, who may treat us in the same manner, and then, where will be our freedom? where our property? As to religion, I hold it to be the indispensable duty of all government, to protect all conscientious professors thereof, and I know of no other business which government has to do therewith. Let a man throw aside that narrowness of soul, that selfishness of principle, which the niggards of all professions are so unwilling to part with, and he will be at delivered of his fears on that head. Suspicion is the companion of mean souls, and the bane of all good society. For myself, I fully and conscientiously believe, that it is the will of the Almighty, that there should be diversity of religious opinions among us: It affords a larger field for our Christian kindness. Were we all of one way of thinking, our religious dispositions would want matter for probation; and on this liberal principle, I look on the various denominations among us, to be like children of the same family, differing only, in what is called, their Christian names.

In page forty, I threw out a few thoughts on the propriety of a Continental Charter, (for I only presume to offer hints, not plans) and in this place, I take the liberty of rementioning the subject, by observing, that a charter is to be understood as a bond of solemn obligation, which the whole enters into, to support the right of every separate part, whether of religion, personal freedom, or property. A firm bargain and a right reckoning make long friends.

In a former page I likewise mentioned the necessity of a large and equal representation; and there is no political matter which more deserves our attention. A small number of electors, or a small number of representatives, are equally dangerous. But if the number of the representatives be not only small, but unequal, the danger is increased. As an instance of this, I mention the following; when the Associators petition was before the House of Assembly of Pennsylvania; twenty-eight members only were present, all the Bucks county members, being eight, voted against it, and had seven of the Chester members done the same, this whole province had been governed by two counties only, and this danger it is always exposed to. The unwarrantable stretch likewise, which that house made in their last sitting, to gain an undue authority over the delegates of that province, ought to warn the people at large, how they trust power out of their own hands. A set of instructions for the Delegates were put together, which in point of sense and business would have dishonoured a schoolboy, and after being approved by a FEW, a VERY FEW without doors, were carried into the House, and there passed IN BEHALF OF THE WHOLE COLONY; whereas, did the whole colony know, with what ill-will that House has entered on some necessary public measures, they would not hesitate a moment to think them unworthy of such a trust.

Immediate necessity makes many things convenient, which if continued would grow into oppressions. Expedience and right are different things. When the calamities of America required a consultation, there was no method so ready, or at that time so proper, as to appoint persons from the several Houses of Assembly for that purpose; and the wisdom with which they have proceeded has preserved this continent from ruin. But as it is more than probable that we shall never be without a CONGRESS, every well wisher to good order, must own, that the mode for choosing members of that body, deserves consideration. And I put it as a question to those, who make a study of mankind, whether representation and election is not too great a power for one and the same body of men to possess? When we are planning for posterity, we ought to remember, that virtue is not hereditary.

It is from our enemies that we often gain excellent maxims, and are frequently surprised into reason by their mistakes, Mr. Cornwall (one of the Lords of the Treasury) treated the petition of the New York Assembly with contempt, because THAT House, he said, consisted but of twenty six members, which trifling number, he argued, could not with decency be put for the whole. We thank him for his involuntary honesty.

TO CONCLUDE, however strange it may appear to some, or however unwilling they may be to think so, matters not, but many strong and striking reasons may be given, to show, that nothing can settle our affairs so expeditiously as an open and determined declaration for independence. Some of which are,

FIRST. — It is the custom of nations, when any two are at war, for some other powers, not engaged in the quarrel, to step in as mediators, and bring about the preliminaries of a peace: but while America calls herself the Subject of Great Britain, no power, however well disposed she may be, can offer her mediation. Wherefore, in our present state we may quarrel on forever.

SECONDLY. — It is unreasonable to suppose, that France or Spain will give us any kind of assistance, if we mean only, to make use of that assistance for the purpose of repairing the breach, and strengthening the connection between Britain and America; because, those powers would be sufferers by the consequences.

THIRDLY. — While we profess ourselves the subjects of Britain, we must, in the eye of foreign nations, be considered as rebels. The precedent is somewhat dangerous to THEIR PEACE, for men to be in arms under the name of subjects; we, on the spot, can solve the paradox: but to unite resistance and subjection, requires an idea much too refined for common understanding.

FOURTHLY. — Were a manifesto to be published, and dispatched to foreign courts, setting forth the miseries we have endured, and the peaceable methods we have ineffectually used for redress; declaring, at the same time, that not being able, any longer, to live happily or safely under the cruel disposition of the British court, we had been driven to the necessity of breaking off all connections with her; at the same time, assuring all such courts of our peaceable disposition towards them, and of our desire of entering into trade with them: Such a memorial would produce more good effects to this Continent, than if a ship were freighted with petitions to Britain.

Under our present denomination of British subjects, we can neither be received nor heard abroad: The custom of all courts is against us, and will be so, until, by an independence, we take rank with other nations.

These proceedings may at first appear strange and difficult; but, like all other steps which we have already passed over, will in a little time become familiar and agreeable; and, until an independence is declared, the Continent will feel itself like a man who continues putting off some unpleasant business from day to day, yet knows it must be done, hates to set about it, wishes it over, and is continually haunted with the thoughts of its necessity.

Appendix

Since the publication of the first edition of this pamphlet, or rather, on the same day on which it came out, the King's Speech made its appearance in this city. Had the spirit of prophecy directed the birth of this production, it could not have brought it forth, at a more seasonable juncture, or a more necessary time. The bloody mindedness of the one, show the necessity of pursuing the doctrine of the other. Men read by way of revenge. And the Speech, instead of terrifying, prepared a way for the manly principles of Independence.

Ceremony, and even, silence, from whatever motive they may arise, have a hurtful tendency, when they give the least degree of countenance to base and wicked performances; wherefore, if this maxim be admitted, it naturally follows, that the King's Speech, as being a piece of finished villainy, deserved, and still deserves, a general execration both by the Congress and the people. Yet, as the domestic tranquility of a nation, depends greatly, on the CHASTITY of what may properly be called NATIONAL MANNERS, it is often better, to pass some things over in silent disdain, than to make use of such new methods of dislike, as might introduce the least innovation, on that guardian of our peace and safety. And, perhaps, it is chiefly owing to this prudent delicacy, that the King's Speech, has not, before now, suffered a public execution. The Speech if it may be called one, is nothing better than a wilful audacious libel against the truth, the common good, and the existence of mankind; and is a formal and pompous method of offering up human sacrifices to the pride of tyrants. But this general massacre of mankind is one of the privileges, and the certain consequence of Kings; for as nature knows them NOT, they know NOT HER, and although they are beings of our OWN creating, they know not US, and have become the gods of their creators. The Speech has one good quality, which is, that it is not calculated to deceive, neither can we, even if we would, be deceived by it. Brutality and tyranny appear on the face of it. It leaves us at no loss: And every line convinces, even in the moment of reading, that He, who hunts the woods for prey, the naked and untutored Indian, is less a Savage than the King of Britain.

Sir John Dalrymple, the putative father of a whining Jesuitical piece, fallaciously called, "THE ADDRESS OF THE PEOPLE OF ENGLAND TO THE INHABITANTS OF AMERICA," has, perhaps, from a vain supposition, that the people here were to be frightened at the pomp and description of a king, given, (though very unwisely on his part) the real character of the present one: "But," says this writer, "if you are inclined to pay compliments to an administration, which we do not complain of(meaning the Marquis of Rockingham's at the repeal of the Stamp Act), it is very unfair in you to withhold them from that prince by WHOSE NOD ALONE THEY WERE PERMITTED TO DO

ANY THING." This is Toryism with a witness! Here is idolatry even without a mask: And he who can calmly hear, and digest such doctrine, has forfeited his claim to rationality; is an apostate from the order of manhood, and ought to be considered as one, who has not only given up the proper dignity of man, but sunk himself beneath the rank of animals, and contemptibly crawl through the world like a worm.

However, it matters very little now, what the king of England either says or does; he has wickedly broken through every moral and human obligation, trampled nature and conscience beneath his feet; and by a steady and constitutional spirit of insolence and cruelty, procured for himself an universal hatred. It is NOW the interest of America to provide for herself. She has already a large and young family, whom it is more her duty to take care of, than to be granting away her property, to support a power who has become a reproach to the names of men and Christians— YOU, whose office it is to watch over the morals of a nation, of whatsoever sect or denomination you are of, as well as you, who, are more immediately the guardians of the public liberty, if you wish to preserve your native country uncontaminated by European corruption, you must in secret wish a separation— But leaving the moral part to private reflection, I shall chiefly confine my farther remarks to the following heads.

First. That it is the interest of America to be separated from Britain.

Secondly. Which is the easiest and most practicable plan, RECONCILIATION OR INDEPENDANCE? With some occasional remarks.

In support of the first, I could, if I judged it proper, produce the opinion of some of the ablest and most experienced men on this continent;

and whose sentiments, on that head, are not yet publicly known. It is in reality a self-evident position: For no nation in a state of foreign dependence, limited in its commerce, and cramped and fettered in its legislative powers, can ever arrive at any material eminence. America does not yet know what opulence is; and although the progress which she has made stands unparalleled in the history of other nations, it is but childhood, compared with what she would be capable of arriving at, had she, as she ought to have, the legislative powers in her own hands. England is, at this time, proudly coveting what would do her no good, were she to accomplish it; and the Continent hesitating on a matter, which will be her final ruin if neglected. It is the commerce and not the conquest of America, by which England is to be benefited, and that would in a great measure continue, were the countries as independent of each other as France and Spain; because in many articles, neither can go to a better market. But it is the independence of this country of Britain or any other, which is now the main and only object worthy of contention, and which, like all other truths discovered by necessity, will appear clearer and stronger every day.

First. Because it will come to that one time or other.

Secondly. Because, the longer it is delayed the harder it will be to accomplish.

I have frequently amused myself both in public and private companies, with silently remarking, the specious errors of those who speak without reflecting. And among the many which I have heard, the following seems the most general, viz. that had this rupture happened forty or fifty years hence, instead of NOW, the Continent would have been more able to have shaken off the dependence. To which I reply, that our military ability, AT THIS TIME, arises from the experience gained in the last war, and which in forty or fifty years time, would have been totally extinct. The Continent, would not, by that time, have had a General, or even a military officer left; and we, or those who may succeed us, would have been as ignorant of martial matters as the ancient Indians: And this single position, closely attended to, will unanswerably prove, that the present time is preferable to all others. The argument turns thus—at the conclusion of the last war, we had experience, but wanted numbers; and forty or fifty years hence, we should have numbers, without experience; wherefore, the proper point of time, must be some particular point between the two extremes, in which a sufficiency of the former remains, and a proper increase of the latter is obtained: And that point of time is the present time.

The reader will pardon this digression, as it does not properly come under the head I first set out with, and to which I again return by the following position, viz.

Should affairs be patched up with Britain, and she to remain the governing and sovereign power of America, (which, as matters are now circumstanced, is giving up the point entirely) we shall deprive ourselves of the very means of sinking the debt we have, or may contract. The value of the back lands which some of the provinces are clandestinely deprived of, by the unjust extension of the limits of Canada, valued only at five pounds sterling per hundred acres, amount to upwards of twenty five millions, Pennsylvania currency; and the quit-rents at one penny sterling per acre, to two million yearly.

It is by the sale of those lands that the debt may be sunk, without burthen to any, and the quit-rent reserved thereon, will always lessen, and in time, will wholly support the yearly expense of government. It matters not how long the debt is in paying, so that the lands when sold be applied to the discharge of it, and for the execution of which, the Congress for the time being, will be the continental trustees.

I proceed now to the second head, viz. Which is the easiest and most practicable plan, RECONCILIATION or INDEPENDANCE; With some occasional remarks.

He who takes nature for his guide is not easily beaten out of his argument, and on that ground, I answer GENERALLY— THAT INDEPENDANCE BEING A SINGLE SIMPLE LINE, CONTAINED WITHIN OURSELVES; AND RECONCILIATION, A MATTER EXCEEDINGLY PERPLEXED AND COMPLICATED, AND IN WHICH, A TREACHEROUS CAPRICIOUS COURT IS TO INTERFERE, GIVES THE ANSWER WITHOUT A DOUBT.

The present state of America is truly alarming to every man who is capable of reflection. Without law, without government, without any other mode of power than what is founded on, and granted by courtesy. Held together by an unexampled concurrence of sentiment, which, is nevertheless subject to change, and which, every secret enemy is endeavouring to dissolve. Our present condition, is, Legislation without law; wisdom without a plan; a constitution without a name; and, what is strangely astonishing, perfect Independence contending for dependence. The instance is without a precedent; the case never existed before; and who can tell what may be the event? The property of no man is secure in the present unbraced system of things. The mind of the multitude is left at random, and seeing no fixed object before them, they pursue such as fancy or opinion starts. Nothing is criminal; there is no such thing as treason; wherefore, everyone thinks himself at liberty to act as he pleases. The Tories dared not have assembled offensively, had they known that their lives, by that act, were forfeited to the laws of the state. A line of distinction should be drawn, between, English soldiers taken in battle, and inhabitants of America taken in arms. The first are prisoners, but the latter traitors. The one forfeits his liberty, the other his head.

Notwithstanding our wisdom, there is a visible feebleness in some of our proceedings which gives encouragement to dissensions. The Continental Belt is too loosely buckled. And if something is not done in time, it will be too late to do anything, and we shall fall into a state, in which, neither RECONCILIATION nor INDEPENDANCE will be practicable. The king and his worthless adherents are got at their old game of dividing the Continent, and there are not wanting among us, Printers, who will be busy in spreading specious falsehoods. The artful and hypocritical letter which appeared a few months ago in two of the New York papers, and likewise in two others, is an evidence that there are men who want either judgment or honesty.

It is easy getting into holes and corners and talking of reconciliation. But do such men seriously consider, how difficult the task is, and how dangerous it may prove, should the Continent divide thereon? Do they take within their view, all the various orders of men whose situation and circumstances, as well as their own, are to be considered therein? Do they put themselves in the place of the sufferer whose ALL is ALREADY gone, and of the soldier, who has quitted ALL for the defense of his country? If their ill judged moderation be suited to their own private situations only, regardless of others, the event will convince them, that "they are reckoning without their Host."

Put us, says some, on the footing we were on in sixty three: To which I answer, the request is not now in the power of Britain to comply with, neither will she propose it; but if it were, and even should be granted, I ask, as a reasonable question, By what means is such a corrupt and faithless court to be kept to its engagements? Another parliament, nay, even the present, may hereafter repeal the obligation, on the pretense, of its being violently obtained, or unwisely granted; and in that case, Where is our redress? — No going to law with nations; cannon are the barristers of Crowns; and the sword, not of justice, but of war, decides the suit. To be on the footing of sixty three, it is not sufficient, that the laws only be put on the same state, but, that our circumstances, likewise, be put on the same state; Our burnt and destroyed towns repaired or built up, our private losses made good, our public debts (contracted for defense) discharged; otherwise, we shall be millions worse than we were at that enviable period. Such a request, had it been complied with a year ago, would have won the heart and soul of the Continent— but now it is too late, "The Rubicon is passed."

Besides, the taking up arms, merely to enforce the repeal of a pecuniary law, seems as unwarrantable by the divine law, and as repugnant to human feelings, as the taking up arms to enforce obedience thereto. The object, on either side, does not justify the means; for the lives of men are too valuable to be cast away on such trifles. It is the violence which is done and threatened to our persons; the destruction of our property by an armed force; the invasion of our country by fire and sword, which conscientiously qualifies the use of arms: And the instant, in which such a mode of defense became necessary, all subjection to Britain ought to have ceased; and the independency of America, should have been considered, as dating its era from, and published by, THE FIRST MUSKET THAT WAS FIRED AGAINST HER. This line is a line of consistency; neither drawn by caprice, nor extended by ambition; but produced by a chain of events, of which the colonies were not the authors.

I shall conclude these remarks with the following timely and well intended hints. We ought to reflect, that there are three different ways by which an independency may hereafter be effected; and that ONE of those THREE, will one day or other, be the fate of America, viz. By the legal voice of the people in Congress; by a military power; or by a mob— It may not always happen that OUR soldiers are citizens, and the multitude a body of reasonable men; virtue, as I have already remarked, is not hereditary, neither is it perpetual. Should an independency be brought about by the first of those means, we have every opportunity and every encouragement before us, to form the noblest purest constitution on the face of the earth. We have it in our power to begin the world over again. A situation, similar to the present, has not happened since the days of Noah until now. The birthday of a new world is at hand, and a race of men, perhaps as numerous as all Europe contains, are to receive their portion of freedom from the event of a few months. The Reflection is awful— and in this point of view, How trifling, how ridiculous, do the little, paltry cavillings, of a few weak or interested men appear, when weighed against the business of a world.

Should we neglect the present favourable and inviting period, and an Independence be hereafter effected by any other means, we must charge the consequence to ourselves, or to those rather, whose narrow and prejudiced souls, are habitually opposing the measure, without

174

either inquiring or reflecting. There are reasons to be given in support of Independence, which men should rather privately think of, than be publicly told of. We ought not now to be debating whether we shall be independent or not, but, anxious to accomplish it on a firm, secure, and honorable basis, and uneasy rather that it is not yet began upon. Every day convinces us of its necessity. Even the Tories (if such beings yet remain among us) should, of all men, be the most solicitous to promote it; for, as the appointment of committees at first, protected them from popular rage, so, a wise and well established form of government, will be the only certain means of continuing it securely to them. WHEREFORE, if they have not virtue enough to be WHIGS, they ought to have prudence enough to wish for Independence.

In short, Independence is the only BOND that can tie and keep us together. We shall then see our object, and our ears will be legally shut against the schemes of an intriguing, as well, as a cruel enemy. We shall then too, be on a proper footing, to treat with Britain; for there is reason to conclude, that the pride of that court, will be less hurt by treating with the American states for terms of peace, than with those, whom she denominates, "rebellious subjects," for terms of accommodation. It is our delaying it that encourages her to hope for conquest, and our backwardness tends only to prolong the war. As we have, without any good effect therefrom, withheld our trade to obtain a redress of our grievances, let us now try the alternative, by independently redressing them ourselves, and then offering to open the trade. The mercantile and reasonable part in England, will be still with us; because, peace with trade, is preferable to war without it. And if this offer be not accepted, other courts may be applied to.

On these grounds I rest the matter. And as no offer has yet been made to refute the doctrine contained in the former editions of this pamphlet, it is a negative proof, that either the doctrine cannot be refuted, or, that the party in favour of it are too numerous to be opposed. WHEREFORE, instead of gazing at each other with suspicious or doubtful curiosity; let each of us, hold out to his neighbour the hearty hand of friendship, and unite in drawing a line, which, like an act of oblivion shall bury in forgetfulness every former dissension. Let the names of Whig and Tory be extinct; and let none other be heard among us, than those of A GOOD CITIZEN, AN OPEN AND RESOLUTE FRIEND, AND A VIRTUOUS SUPPORTER OF THE RIGHTS OF MANKIND AND OF THE FREE AND INDEPENDANT STATES OF AMERICA.

To the Representatives of the Religious Society of the People called Quakers, or to so many of them as were concerned in publishing the late piece, entitled "THE ANCIENT TESTIMONY and PRINCIPLES of the People called QUAKERS renewed, with Respect to the KING and GOVERNMENT, and touching the COMMOTIONS now prevailing in these and other parts of AMERICA addressed to the PEOPLE IN GENERAL."

The Writer of this, is one of those few, who never dishonours religion either by ridiculing, or cavilling at any denomination whatsoever. To God, and not to man, are all men accountable on the score of religion. Wherefore, this epistle is not so properly addressed to you as a religious, but as a political body, dabbling in matters, which the professed Quietude of your Principles instruct you not to meddle with. As you have, without a proper authority for so doing, put yourselves in the place of the whole body of the Quakers, so, the writer of this, in order to be on an equal rank with yourselves, is under the necessity, of putting himself in the place of all those, who, approve the very writings and principles, against which, your testimony is directed: And he has chosen this singular situation, in order, that you might discover in him that presumption of character which you cannot see in yourselves. For neither he nor you can have any claim or title to POLITICAL REPRESENTATION.

When men have departed from the right way, it is no wonder that they stumble and fall. And it is evident from the manner in which you have managed your testimony, that politics, (as a religious body of men) is not your proper Walk; for however well adapted it might appear to you, it is, nevertheless, a jumble of good and bad put unwisely together, and the conclusion drawn therefrom, both unnatural and unjust.

The two first pages, (and the whole does not make four) we give you credit for, and expect the same civility from you, because the love and desire of peace is not confined to Quakerism, it is the natural, as well the religious wish of all denominations of men. And on this ground, as men labouring to establish an Independent Constitution of our own, do we exceed all others in our hope, end, and aim. OUR PLAN IS PEACE FOREVER. We are tired of contention with Britain, and can see no real end to it but in a final separation. We act consistently, because for the sake of introducing an endless and uninterrupted peace, do we bear the evils and burdens of the present day. We are endeavoring, and will steadily continue to endeavour, to separate and dissolve a connection which has already filled our land with blood; and which, while the name of it remains, will be the fatal cause of future mischiefs to both countries. We fight neither for revenge nor conquest; neither from pride nor passion; we are not insulting the world with our fleets and armies, nor ravaging the globe for plunder. Beneath the shade of our own vines are we attacked; in our own houses, and on our own lands, is the violence committed against us. We view our enemies in the character of Highwaymen and Housebreakers, and having no defense for ourselves in the civil law, are obliged to punish them by the military one, and apply the sword, in the very case, where you have before now, applied the halter— Perhaps we feel for the ruined and insulted sufferers in all and every part of the continent, with a degree of tenderness which has not yet made its way into some of your bosoms. But be you sure that you mistake not the cause and ground of your Testimony. Call not coldness of soul, religion; nor put the BIGOT in the place of the CHRISTIAN.

O you partial ministers of your own acknowledged principles. If the bearing arms be sinful, the first going to war must be more so, by all the difference between wilful attack, and unavoidable defense. Wherefore, if you really preach from conscience, and mean not to make a political hobbyhorse of your religion, convince the world thereof, by proclaiming your doctrine to our enemies, FOR THEY LIKEWISE BEAR ARMS. Give us proof of your sincerity by publishing it at St. James's, to the commanders in chief at Boston, to the Admirals and Captains who are piratically ravaging our coasts, and to all the murdering miscreants who are acting in authority under HIM whom you profess to serve. Had you the honest soul of BARCLAY you would preach repentance to YOUR king; You would tell the Royal Wretch his sins, and warn him of eternal ruin. You would not spend your partial invectives against the injured and the insulted only, but, like faithful ministers, would cry aloud and SPARE NONE. Say not that you are persecuted, neither endeavour to make us the authors of that reproach, which, you are bringing upon

178

yourselves; for we testify unto all men, that we do not complain against you because you are Quakers, but because you pretend to be and are NOT Quakers.

Alas! it seems by the particular tendency of some part of your testimony, and other parts of your conduct, as if, all sin was reduced to, and comprehended in, THE ACT OF BEARING ARMS, and that by the people only. You appear to us, to have mistaken party for conscience; because, the general tenor of your actions wants uniformity— And it is exceedingly difficult to us to give credit to many of your pretended scruples; because, we see them made by the same men, who, in the very instant that they are exclaiming against the mammon of this world, are nevertheless, hunting after it with a step as steady as Time, and an appetite as keen as Death.

The quotation which you have made from Proverbs, in the third page of your testimony, that, "when a man's ways please the Lord, he makes even his enemies to be at peace with him"; is very unwisely chosen on your part; because, it amounts to a proof, that the king's ways (whom you are desirous of supporting) do NOT please the Lord, otherwise, his reign would be in peace.

I now proceed to the latter part of your testimony, and that, for which all the foregoing seems only an introduction viz.

"It has ever been our judgment and principle, since we were called to profess the light of Christ Jesus, manifested in our consciences unto this day, that the setting up and putting down kings and governments, is God's peculiar prerogative; for causes best known to himself: And that it is not our business to have any hand or contrivance therein; nor to be busy bodies above our station, much less to plot and contrive the ruin, or overturn of any of them, but to pray for the king, and safety of our nation, and good of all men— That we may live a peaceable and quiet life, in all godliness and honesty; UNDER THE GOVERNMENT WHICH GOD IS PLEASED TO SET OVER US"— If these are REALLY your principles why do you not abide by them? Why do you not leave that, which you call God's Work, to be managed by himself? These very principles instruct you to wait with patience and humility, for the event of all public measures, and to receive that event as the divine will towards you. Wherefore, what occasion is there for your POLITICAL TESTIMONY if you fully believe what it contains? And the very publishing it proves, that either, you do not believe what you profess, or have not virtue enough to practise what you believe.

The principles of Quakerism have a direct tendency to make a man the quiet and inoffensive subject of any, and every government WHICH IS SET OVER HIM. And if the setting up and putting down of kings and governments is God's peculiar prerogative, he most certainly will not be robbed thereof by us: wherefore, the principle itself leads you to approve of everything, which ever happened, or may happen to kings as being his work. OLIVER CROMWELL thanks you. CHARLES, then, died not by the hands of man; and should the present Proud Imitator of him, come to the same untimely end, the writers and publishers of the Testimony, are bound, by the doctrine it contains, to applaud the fact. Kings are not taken away by miracles, neither are changes in governments brought about by any other means than such as are common and human; and such as we are now using. Even the dispersion of the Jews, though foretold by our Saviour, was effected by arms. Wherefore, as you refuse to be the means on one side, you ought not to be meddlers on the other; but to wait the issue in silence; and unless you can produce divine authority, to prove, that the Almighty who has created and placed this new world, at the greatest distance it could possibly stand, east and west, from every part of the old, does, nevertheless, disapprove of its being independent of the corrupt and abandoned court of Britain, unless I say, you can show this, how can you on the ground of your principles, justify the exciting and stirring up the people "firmly to unite in the abhorrence of all such writings, and measures, as evidence a desire and design to break off the happy connection we have hitherto enjoyed, with the kingdom of Great—Britain, and our just and necessary subordination to the king, and those who are lawfully placed in authority under him." What a slap of the face is here! the men, who in the very paragraph before, have quietly and passively resigned up the ordering, altering, and disposal of kings and governments, into the hands of God, are now, recalling their principles, and putting in for a share of the business. Is it possible, that the conclusion, which is here justly quoted, can any ways follow from the doctrine laid down? The inconsistency is too glaring not to be seen; the absurdity too great not to be laughed at; and such as could only have been made by those, whose understandings were darkened by the narrow and crabby spirit of a despairing political party; for you are not to be considered as the whole body of the Quakers but only as a factional and fractional part thereof.

Here ends the examination of your testimony; (which I call upon no man to abhor, as you have done, but only to read and judge of fairly;) to which I subjoin the following remark; "That the setting up and putting down of kings," most certainly mean, the making him a king, who is yet not so, and the making him no king who is already one. And pray what has this to do in the present case? We neither mean to set up nor to pull down, neither to make nor to unmake, but to have nothing to do with them. Wherefore, your testimony in whatever light it is viewed serves only to dishonor your judgement, and for many other reasons had better have been let alone than published.

First, Because it tends to the decrease and reproach of all religion whatever, and is of the utmost danger to society to make it a party in political disputes.

Secondly, Because it exhibits a body of men, numbers of whom disavow the publishing political testimonies, as being concerned therein and approvers thereof.

Thirdly, because it has a tendency to undo that continental harmony and friendship which yourselves by your late liberal and charitable donations has lent a hand to establish; and the preservation of which, is of the utmost consequence to us all.

And here without anger or resentment I bid you farewell. Sincerely wishing, that as men and Christians, you may always fully and uninterruptedly enjoy every civil and religious right; and be, in your turn, the means of securing it to others; but that the example which you have unwisely set, of mingling religion with politics, MAY BE DISAVOWED AND REPROBATED BY EVERY INHABITANT OF AMERICA.